"**W**hat am I doing naked in this bed with you?" Duke asked.

Marnie felt her cheeks burn as she glanced down at his bare chest and remembered. "You fell overboard, and I pulled you out and put you to bed. I'll make some coffee and fill you in on the details."

"You kissed me, Marnie, didn't you? In this bed."

She recalled how she'd kissed him to keep him quiet, and knew what she'd felt for him then was nothing compared to what she'd feel if he were to kiss her now. For he was sober and in control and looking handsomer than any man had a right to look with his tousled hair, his twenty-four hour beard, and his sexy, hair-matted chest. "Yes, I kissed you," she whispered.

"But nothing else happened."

"How can you be so certain of that?"

"Because if we'd made love, you wouldn't be wearing clothes, and you wouldn't be looking at me with so much speculation in your eyes. . . ."

WHAT ARE *LOVESWEPT* ROMANCES?

They are stories of true romance and touching emotion. We believe those two very important ingredients are constants in our highly sensual and very believable stories in the LOVESWEPT *line. Our goal is to give you, the reader, stories of consistently high quality that may sometimes make you laugh, sometimes make you cry, but are always fresh and creative and contain many delightful surprises within their pages.*

Most romance fans read an enormous number of books. Those they truly love, they keep. Others may be traded with friends and soon forgotten. We hope that each LOVESWEPT *romance will be a treasure—a "keeper." We will always try to publish*

LOVE STORIES YOU'LL NEVER FORGET BY AUTHORS YOU'LL ALWAYS REMEMBER

The Editors

Loveswept® 630

BELIEVING HEART

LYNNE BRYANT

BANTAM BOOKS

NEW YORK · TORONTO · LONDON · SYDNEY · AUCKLAND

BELIEVING HEART

A Bantam Book / August 1993

If you would be interested in receiving protective vinyl covers for your
Loveswept books, please write to this address for information:

> Loveswept
> Bantam Books
> P.O. Box 985
> Hicksville, NY 11802

ISBN 0-553-44253-8

Published simultaneously in the United States and Canada

Bantam Books are published by Bantam Books, a division of Bantam Doubleday Dell Publishing Group, Inc. Its trademark, consisting of the words
"Bantam Books" and the portrayal of a rooster, is Registered in U.S. Patent
and Trademark Office and in other countries. Marca Registrada. Bantam
Books, 1540 Broadway, New York, New York 10036.

For Darlene and Allan—
may the wind be always at your backs.

BELIEVING HEART

ONE

"Psst! Over here," Marnie MacBride called softly as she stepped up onto the deck of her thirty-two-foot ketch.

The tall man, dressed in black from the toes of his highly polished boots to his Stetson, stopped, shook his head, and looked around at the sailboats and power yachts that were berthed along the pier.

"Over here," Marnie called again, more urgently this time, as she moved to the railing of the *Wayward Wind*.

Catching sight of her, the man half turned and staggered toward the sailboat.

"You mean me?" He pointed a long finger at himself, but it missed and wagged over his shoulder.

At any other time Marnie would have laughed at the comical expression on his handsome face, but the protesters she'd seen in the pub a half hour earlier weren't in a humorous mood. In fact, she was sure one of them had slipped something into the man's drink, and if she knew them, they'd be right on his tail. It was a miracle he'd gotten so far with his aristocratic nose still intact.

Marnie stepped lightly onto the floating pier. It wobbled, making the tall man wobble, and she caught his arm to steady him. "Yes, you, Mr. Duke King."

"Do I know you?" He weaved forward, caught himself, then peered into her face. "Ah, yesh. The slady wish the sunset hair and shea-green eyes. The very beautiful slady."

His Stetson was pulled down on his forehead, shielding his eyes, but the admiration in his voice waylaid Marnie. She hadn't realized Duke had noticed her at the conference that morning. Maybe there was hope for her yet, she thought before the clang of the marina gate and the sound of angry male voices jerked her back to reality. The protesters had arrived.

Slipping her arm through Duke's, she pulled him toward her boat. "Come with me. Quickly."

"You want me, ma'am? You can have me," he said, sweeping off his Stetson and bowing low. He would have kept right on going headfirst into the water, if she hadn't pulled him erect. His eyes were the same color as the day that had just passed, she noticed. Autumn, rainy-day gray. A sad, melancholy color that tugged at her heart.

"Oh, for heaven's sake. Just get aboard," she said, propelling the loose-limbed man with the heart-wrenching eyes toward the *Wayward Wind*.

Even drunk, Duke was a man most women would cast bait for, Marnie thought as she helped him crawl over the lifelines onto the teak deck. But she preferred a man who smiled. And she had learned one very important thing while she'd watched him chair the supposedly top-secret gathering of oilmen: Duke King never smiled. He was a man of steel who had controlled the proceedings with an iron hand and an even temper—despite the rudeness of the fishermen and environmentalists who had crashed the oil conference. And he hadn't shown a moment of poor judgment until he'd gone into the pub alone afterward for a drink.

"Yo-ho-ho and a bottle of rum," Duke sang, grinning up at her from his half-sitting perch on the edge of the cockpit as she climbed nimbly aboard. With another flourish he settled his Stetson on top of his thick raven-black hair and began to sing again. "Yo-ho—"

"Shhh. Please, just go below and be quiet." She glanced anxiously over her shoulder and breathed a sigh of relief when she discovered the protesters still weren't in sight. "You're in danger. Some men are out to get you."

"Who? Where? Let me at them." He stood upright and staggered. She caught him and levered him to the top of the companionway, but he stumbled and fell down the three steps. Marnie followed him, carefully avoiding his sprawled body as she pulled the hatch closed.

A kerosene lamp glowed warmly against the rich cedar hull. The oilman lay on the floor, propped up on one elbow, watching her. Silently. Most men would be cursing a blue streak . . . but not Mr. No-Emotion King.

"Are you all right? Did you hurt yourself when you fell?"

"I'm dying," he said, dramatically placing a hand over his heart. "For you."

"Maybe I should leave you to your fate," she muttered as she picked up his Stetson and set it down in the galley to the right of the companionway. Switching on the battery radio, Marnie quickly found a Seattle rock station and turned up the volume. "But if the rumblings I overheard in the pub come true," she continued, keeping her voice low, "your fate could include a severe beating, tar and feathers, or being kidnapped and left on a deserted San Juan Island. King Oil is not well liked in these parts."

"So you decided to kidnap me yourself?" he asked as he slowly sat up. "I kinda cotton to that idea."

"Me! Kidnap you? Now why would I want to do that?" Marnie asked, then decided it might not be a half-bad idea. She had come to Raynaird Resort because she wanted to talk to King. However, now that she had him, he wasn't in any shape to listen to her or remember her request.

"But I'd better hide you before you *do* get kidnapped," she continued as she glanced around the stripped-down salon. Giving a sigh of resignation, she leaned over and extended her hand. "Come on. The only place I can hide you is in the forward berth."

"I like the sound of this more'n'more," he said, taking her hand and rising to his feet with surprising grace and speed.

"Watch your—"

"Ouch!" he said softly as he cracked his head on a beam.

"—noggin," she finished. "How tall are you?"

Gingerly, he rubbed his bent head. "Six-two."

"Well, don't try to stand up straight anywhere in the cabin. There's not enough room," she said, nudging him toward the bow.

He paused in the doorway, looking at the berth that took up the entire forward cabin. Covered with a blue quilt and lined with plump gold and blue pillows, it was classy, elegant, and very plush. "Man, now this is what I call a bed! There's enough room to have an orgy in here."

"Just be thankful there is a bed," she muttered as she watched Duke stretch his long, slim body out on it. She sat down on the edge of the berth and began pulling the cushions around him, thinking she could hide him under them if the men started searching the boat.

He began to sing softly.

"Can't you just be quiet?" she asked, wishing it were another time and place, and she could listen to him sing. His voice was a beautiful, rich tenor, perfect for singing love songs.

For a moment he looked disappointed, almost hurt, then his face became hard, his eyes cold and bleak. "Why? Don't you like my voice?"

"Your voice is beautiful, and I would love to hear you sing, but they're coming down the docks, searching for you. Can't you hear them?" She leaned across him to reach for a pillow.

"I can only hear the beat of my heart. And yours."

His hand was firm but gentle as it touched her breast. Her nipple hardened instantly in response, and Marnie drew back and stared down at him in surprise. This couldn't be happening to her, she thought in amazement. Never before had a man made her feel so sensitive, so breathless, so . . . full of tension by merely touching her. He continued to cup her breast, and she continued to gaze at him, wondering if he could hear her heart, which was thumping like a loose sail in a gale.

Duke smiled slightly and began to sing again.

The sound of his voice reminded Marnie that she should be thinking of more important things, such as keeping him safe. With a sigh of exasperation, she leaned forward and silenced him by the very simple method of placing her lips against his.

Oh dear, oh dear, oh dear. He wasn't supposed to have such warm lips, Marnie thought in semi-panic. His kiss wasn't supposed to scorch her toes. Wasn't supposed to make her blood sing like the wind in the rigging. Wasn't supposed to make her feel so feminine, so desirable . . . and so needy.

Why didn't she feel this way when she kissed Gil Green? she wondered, suddenly guilty because she was kissing Duke when she was considering marrying her father's foreman. Shaken by the unwanted memory, she rolled away from Duke and pressed her hands to her breast, where her heart was still misbehaving.

Duke turned on his side to look at her. "Lord, but a man can get drunk on your kisses," he said huskily, his gray eyes silvered with desire.

"You're already drunk," she whispered.

"Doesn't matter."

Snaking out his arm, he pulled her back on top of him and began kissing her again as if he hadn't kissed a woman in a long time. As if he had years of wanting and needing locked up inside him, waiting for release.

The need knocked on her heart, begging to be heard, but she refused to listen, admonishing herself that she should be thinking of Gil. She struggled to free herself, but when Duke started to protest, she changed her mind and pressed her lips against his to shush him once more. She could easily become addicted to shushing Duke, she thought. His lips were tantalizing, persuasive, seductive. And his oh-so-powerful body was a work of art. All hard, clean lines and graceful movements . . . like a racing sloop, but much more sexy.

His hands were warm as he slipped them under her sweater, his fingertips smooth as he began caressing the sides of her breasts. Her response was just as fast, but ten times stronger than before, flooding her whole body with desire. And the desire continued to build as he caressed her.

"There's buried treasure somewhere under this sweater," he murmured. "And I'm going to find it."

His words woke Marnie from the spell his hands and his kisses had woven around her. "Oh no, you're not," she said, pulling away from him abruptly.

He reached for her again, but she stopped him with a don't-you-dare-touch-me glare. "No?" he asked in disappointment.

Marnie shook her head, wondering why she had let him take so many liberties. She didn't want or need this, she told herself sternly. Not when she already had another needy man to worry about.

Duke gazed at her a moment longer, then slowly the silver faded from his eyes, leaving them cold and hard as flint. "You're as-absolutely right," he said softly. "I don't even know your name. S-Say, what is your name?"

"Marnie. Marnie MacBride."

"Marnie . . . Marnie of the sea." He closed his eyes and sighed. "I think I'll dream of you for a while, sea witch, because suddenly I feel very . . ."

Slowly, Marnie sat up, slid to the foot of the berth, and gazed down at him, still shaken by the feelings he had aroused in her.

Why were his eyes so cold, she wondered, when his lips were so warm?

The sound of voices coming closer intruded into her thoughts, and she quickly covered Duke with pillows, admitting even as she worked that it was useless. The men would spot him in two shakes, if they ever searched the boat. But she wasn't about to let them on board, she vowed as she silently crossed the main cabin and crouched beside the companionway.

"Where in blazes did he get to?"

"Canna gone fir after those knockout drops you put in his drink. They be strong enough to down an ox. Maybe he fell in the water and drowned."

"Hell, I hope not," a third man spoke up. "Maybe he crawled onto one of the boats. Let's search them."

"Bloody good idea. We'll start with *Wayward Wind*. MacBride, you in there?"

The voice galvanized Marnie into action. Blowing out the lamp, she pulled back the hatch partway and eased through the small opening to stand on the top step of the companionway. "What's the matter, boys?" she asked the three men standing on the dock.

A burly man whose beer-belly stretched his sweater to the limits came closer. "Who do ya got down there with ya?"

"Just me and my radio. Why?" Marnie asked, recognizing the man. Sampson had a reputation in the islands for being a hotheaded bully, and the stint in the pub had only served to increase his temper and loosen his tongue. In fact, none of the men seemed to care who knew they were after Duke.

"We're looking for King. Have you bloody well seen him?" asked the second man, Booring. The tall man dressed in dirty jeans and plaid jacket was Haigen, an activist from England, Marnie knew, and the man who had spearheaded the ruckus at the meeting. The fact that he was packing what looked like a pistol in his jacket pocket made her shiver.

"What do you want him for, Booring?"

"Nothing you should be worrying your pretty little head about," Haigen answered, giving her a leer that sent more shivers down her spine. The flimsy lock on her hatch wouldn't keep him out if he decided to come calling, and she wouldn't put it past him to decide to do just that.

And there was no one else in the marina to come to her aid if she needed help. No one to come to Duke's aid.

"Have you seen my cat?" Marnie asked, coming to a sudden decision.

As she had hoped, her question seemed to catch them off guard. "Your cat? Whadda ya want your cat for?" Sampson asked, scratching his belly.

"Because I got what I came for and I'm leaving," she said, fear making her voice sharper and louder than normal. "Here, Clarence. Here, Clarence."

Booring peered at her suspiciously. "You can't go sailing off in the middle of the bloody night."

"There's a full moon, and the wind is right, so it will only take me a couple of hours to get home," she said, then called the cat again, praying that for once Clarence would forget he was such an independent cuss and come when he was called.

There was a streak of yellow on the dock and a thud as the cat hit the foredeck. Marnie breathed a sigh of relief. "Come here, you old reprobate," she said softly, and leaned forward to pick up the cat as he hopped along the top of the cabin. After giving his ragged ears a quick scratch, she dropped him inside, snagged her floater jacket from a hook on the companionway, and scrambled out, pulling the hatch shut behind her.

"Stand by to cast me off, will you?" she asked as she zipped up her jacket and began removing the sail cover from the aft sail. By the time the men had untied the lines, she had the sail up. Giving them a salute, she took the boat out of the marina. Clear of the markers, she raised the other sails, then settled back to enjoy the ride home to the MacBride Boatyard on nearby San Juan Island.

Thank goodness the full moon lit her passage, because there was nowhere else to go. Raynaird Resort sat in the only sheltered bay on this privately owned island. Thickly wooded mountains dropped straight into the sea, and outcroppings of jagged rocks, some partly submerged, some completely covered by the twelve-foot tide, littered the shoreline. Twenty-five years of sailing had given Marnie a healthy respect for these waters.

Twenty-five years of sailing had also given her a tremendous freedom. Nothing gave her more pleasure than to feel the tiller come alive in her hand, hear the wind humming through the rigging, taste the salt spray on her lips. Her happiness would be complete if only she had a husband who shared her love of the sea and who also loved her—didn't just need her.

"So, a sea witch did kidnap me, after all," Duke said as he crawled out of the companionway into the cockpit.

Marnie smiled at him, then frowned when he slipped. "Sit down before you fall overboard," she said, wishing she had a pair of deck shoes that would fit him. The soles of his boots were dangerously slippery.

"Yes'm."

He sat down next to the aft mast, splayed his legs wide, and propped an arm over the roof of the cabin, looking so relaxed and sexy that Marnie couldn't take her eyes off him. The wind ruffled his thick, perfectly cut black hair, tossing it over his forehead in wicked disarray; the moonlight played over the planes of his face, making him look dangerous and exciting and handsome.

"Doesn't it concern you that I've kidnapped you?" she asked, using his words. When he was sober, she'd tell him why she had sailed out of the marina. And hope he would believe her.

He frowned, considering her question, then shook his head. "Naw. It's about time I had some excitement in my life. My brother Dare has one exciting adventure after another. And even my little brother, Dev, kicked over the traces. Me, all I do is stay at home and run the business."

"You must be doing a pretty good job. From what I hear, it's bad times in Texas right now, and at least King Oil hasn't gone under."

"Yeah, but it has meant keeping my nose to the grindstone."

"And an eye on the clock," she said, remembering the reason she hadn't approached Duke at the conference. After watching him run a no-nonsense meeting, she'd decided he wouldn't give her the time of day, much less the time to listen to her proposition. Especially when she'd forgotten to bring along the formal proposal. An oversight that would be very difficult to explain to a successful businessman.

"To hell with the clock," Duke said, waving his arm in the air. "Who cares about time when I've been shanghaied by a beautiful pirate who sails off with me into the moonlit night? This is high adventure. This is real romance."

"Don't tell me you haven't had any romance in your life either?"

"Nope."

Marnie gazed at Duke, thinking it was kind of sad that he felt he hadn't had any romance in his life. Not that she could believe him. He was so handsome, with his windswept hair and silver-gray eyes, that women must be jumping ship to get at him. And even if he did need a bit of romance, she wasn't about to give it to him. She was having enough trouble deciding what to do about Gil's proposal without adding further complications.

Suddenly, Duke laughed, then stopped abruptly with a surprised look on his face, and then laughed again.

Marnie smiled at him. His laugh was husky, almost rusty. "What's so funny?" she asked.

He sobered and wiped his hand over his face. "I never laugh," he said, and promptly cracked up again.

"Then it's about time you did," she said, laughing with him. "By the sounds of things you needed to laugh. But what's so funny?" she asked again when he finally stopped and dropped his head into his hands.

"Ooooh . . . that hurts," he said, and moaned, sucking in a shaky breath as he raised his head. "When I woke up, I . . . I thought a one-eyed, three-legged . . ." He sat up straight, and she began to grin in anticipation. "A one-eyed, three-legged cat was s-sitting on m-my face."

Marnie giggled. "That was Clarence, my attack cat."

"Then I wasn't having hallucinations." He nodded his head, gingerly. "I must be sober."

"I'll reserve judgment on that," she said. Remembering the conversation she'd overheard among the protesters, she marveled at his constitution. After the Mickey Finn they'd slipped him, he should be spending the rest of the night under the sheets. "I really think you should go below and lie down again."

"And miss all this? A beautiful woman. A full moon. The wind in the sails."

"Well, watch your head, because the sails are coming about," she warned, and prepared to tack. He moved to help her, but she warned him off. "Stay put. I have everything under control. You'll just get in the way."

Settling back, he nodded in admiration. "You're a pretty good sailor."

"For a woman?"

"Naw. For a sailor."

"Well, I should be. I've been sailing since I was five. My father builds boats."

"Did he build this one?"

"No. I did. To be more accurate, I'm restoring it."

"Beautiful." He gazed at her, his hooded eyes making it very plain that he was talking about her, and Marnie felt her cheeks burn despite the cool night air. Finally, he gave her a small smile and stood up.

"Where are you going?" she asked in concern.

He waved toward the bow of the boat. "Up there. I feel like howling at the moon."

"Duke, please sit down." He shook his head, and she shook hers in exasperation as she continued, "At least put on a life jacket. I won't be responsible if you fall overboard. This isn't the Gulf Coast, you know. You won't last more than five minutes in that frigid water."

Just then a wave broke the bow, and the cold spray hit Duke square in the face. He coughed, sputtered, and wiped his face on the sleeve of his sweater. "You made your point."

"The life jackets are down below. And while you're at it, would you turn off the radio?" she asked, hoping that once he was in the warm cabin, he'd fall asleep again before he remembered why he was there.

She had underestimated his self-control, because Mickey Finn or not, he returned immediately, wearing a life jacket. Giving a sigh of resignation, she fished a line out of the locker, then leaned forward and began wrapping the safety harness around his chest.

"Ah, so you want to snuggle, do you?" he asked, snaking his arms around her and pulling her up against his hard chest.

The feel of his body made her knees go weak, her toes curl, her control crumble, and she uttered a sharp warning that was meant more for herself than for him. "Behave!"

"Not even a little kiss?"

"There's nothing little about your kisses," she said, remembering all too vividly the potent ones they'd shared. Pulling out of his arms, she moved back to stand by the tiller. "You'll have to put on the rest of the harness yourself."

He looked over his shoulder at the strap dangling behind him, then looked back at her and raised a sardonic eyebrow. "Chicken?"

"I wouldn't want to be accused of taking liberties with my prisoner," she joked, thinking she would die first rather than pull the strap up between his legs.

"You mean you didn't kidnap me to keep me as a sex slave?" he asked, standing legs apart, hands on hips.

She took a deep breath, trying to steady her flip-flopping stomach, then reached out and touched his arm. "Please humor me, Duke. If you were knocked unconscious and fell into the water, there's no way I could lift you back on board without help. I'm feeling guilty enough about bringing you out here in your condition. I'd never forgive myself if something happened to you."

He frowned down at her. "You're worried about me?"

"I most certainly am."

"No one ever worries about me."

"I know. You're a big, strong macho man, and you don't need anyone to look after you, but please do what I ask." She gave his arm another squeeze before she released it.

"Okay, I'll wear it," he said, pulling the strap up and tying it into the ring. Then he moved closer. "But I still expect a kiss."

"You take bribes?"

"Never." He gave her a wicked grin just before he bent to capture her lips. "I extract payment."

His kiss shook Marnie so badly, she forgot to mind the sails until a gust of wind tilted the boat over, throwing Duke onto the bench on the low side of the cockpit. Marnie grabbed him with one hand and held on to the tiller with the other, gradually bringing the boat back under control.

"Woo-wee. Now that's what I call a kiss," Duke said.

It most definitely was, Marnie thought, fighting to bring her body under control too. Her knees were still trembling, her heart was still pounding, and her senses were still swimming. What was there about this man that attracted her? she wondered. Duke King was definitely a dangerous man, and she was beginning to wish she had left him on shore.

He rose to his feet, dropped another kiss on her lips, and before she could even utter a protest, began weaving his way through the cockpit.

"Where are you going?" she asked, as he started

to crawl over the roof of the cabin. She might be harboring second thoughts about bringing him on board, but she certainly didn't want to have to fish him out of the sea.

"To howl at the moon. After that kiss I feel like howling more than ever."

Quickly, she fastened the end of his safety line to the boat. "Be careful. Your boots are slippery."

"Yes, ma'am," he said as he wrapped his arm around the mainmast and leaned out into the wind.

Marnie caught her breath and prayed the wind would hold, then watched in delight as the tall black pirate threw back his head and began serenading her with a lusty song from *The Pirates of Penzance*. Finishing it, he swung out from the mast again, then broke into another song. For the first time in her life Marnie found herself wishing she could sing, so she could join in with him. And she also found herself thinking that she was very happy she had taken Duke aboard. Dangerous or not, she wouldn't have missed the experience of being serenaded by Duke for all the stars in the sky above. It was far better than her most romantic daydream.

"I don't sing, you know," he called to her when it was over.

"You don't? What have you been doing for the last five minutes?" she asked, completely enthralled.

"Singing," he said, then gave a short laugh of amazement. "I haven't done that for a long time."

"Well, sing some more. I'm enjoying it immensely. But please come down, so I can hear you better."

Surprisingly, he crawled back into the cockpit. A moment later Marnie was wondering if it had been such a hot idea, as he cuddled up close and put his arm around her.

"Is that better?" he asked, smiling into her startled eyes.

They grew even wider when she realized this was the first time he had really smiled at her. All his other smiles had been tight. This was warm and wide and wonderful . . . and did things to her insides that were sinful. Giving him a slight shove, she pushed him down on the bench.

"Sing," she commanded.

"Aye, aye, Captain," he said, and began singing a soft sea chanty that soon brought tears to her eyes.

Absently, she brushed them away and gazed at his face, studying the strength of his jaw, his beautifully sculptured cheekbones, and the elegant bridge of his nose. But it was his eyes that held her captive. Steel-gray eyes that had once looked so cold were now alive with quicksilver.

Abruptly, he stopped singing and laughed. "I'm rusty. Did you hear my voice squeak on that note? I'll have to try it again. Do, re, mi, fa . . ." He continued up the scales until he hit the high note he'd missed. "There. I found you, G-sharp. You can't hide from me any longer. Now . . ." And he broke into song again.

As Duke sang, Marnie began wondering if she was really sailing off into the moonlight with a handsome, sexy dreamboat of a man? Was he really singing love songs . . . to her? And was this magical moonlit night ever going to end?

Zeus! It was going to end right now, Marnie realized moments later as they tacked to clear the mouth of the sound and she saw the bank of black clouds on the strait. A gale was coming right for them.

"Duke, are you sober?" she asked, her voice sharp with concern.

TWO

Duke stopped singing and smiled at Marnie. She had to be the prettiest little lady he'd seen in ages, he thought, admiring the way the moonlight turned her hair into a river of golden fire. She stood on the bucking boat, riding it easily, serenely, looking as if she had just risen out of the sea.

"Duke, are you sober?" she asked again.

"Sober? How can a man be sober when he's drunk on moonlight and a beautiful goddess of the sea?"

"Duke, this is serious. Have you ever sailed a boat?"

The concern in her voice penetrated his happy thoughts. "I'm a landlubber. Why?"

"Because there's a gale-force wind coming straight at us, and you'll have to handle the tiller while I go forward and take down the sails."

"Lord help us," he muttered as he moved to her side.

Hand on the tiller, Duke suddenly became acutely aware of the power of the wind in the sails. "If this isn't gale force, what is it?" he called out to Marnie, who was quickly scrambling forward.

"This is a little warning from Zeus," Marnie yelled back. "Remember, I'm putting my life in your hands."

Duke fought the fog in his brain, wishing he were alert enough to do the dangerous work. Wishing he could put his life in Marnie's hands, because right now she could keep him safer than he could keep her.

"Put on a lifeline," he hollered, and breathed a sigh of relief when he saw she had already tethered herself to the mast.

Marnie clung to the mast, watching him battle the tiller while the wind tore at her, trying to wrench her free. Then she felt the change in the boat, felt the control Duke now had over it. He was handling the helm like a real buccaneer . . . as if he'd been born before the mast, she thought as she began working on the sails. And soon the job was done.

"I thought you were a landlubber," she said, giving him a smile as she took over the tiller once more.

Pleased, he smiled back, wondering when he had last felt so strongly about a woman. "We made a hell of a team, didn't we?"

"We sure did," she said, thinking that he looked almost boyish when he smiled and wondering how she could keep that wide smile on his face.

"Where are we going, anyway?" he asked.

She pointed to a small mountain ahead of them. "We're going to take shelter next to that island over there. We may make it before we lose the moonlight."

The full force of the gale hit them then, knocking at the sails.

"Go below, Duke," she yelled, brushing the wind-whipped hair out of her eyes so she could see.

"No way. I'm staying with—yeow!" he yelled, as a wave splashed over the side of the boat and onto his head.

"I'm sorry I brought you out here," she cried as she fought the tiller. "This storm wasn't due for another two days."

"Take it easy. It's all right," he said, trying to reassure her. Despite the fact that the bow was kissing the clouds one moment and diving into the deep the next, he was certain that they would survive. The little goddess of the sea knew her business.

"Zeus! What am I saying? You're not in any danger out here with me. I've weathered worse storms than this. Besides, you were in more danger back at the marina."

"*What?*" Another wave drenched them, and for the next ten minutes Marnie was too busy to answer his question. When he pitched in and started pulling on the ropes, she let him—after a stern warning to watch his fingers on the winches.

The tiny island came up on their bow, and moments later Marnie tacked, aiming for the mouth of the small inlet and safety. Duke watched the waves splash high on the cliffs to the port, and the rocks flash by on the starboard side as they swept through the narrow gap and into the sheltered water of the inlet.

"We made it!" he yelled, then felt foolish because suddenly the wind no longer howled in his ears, nor did the waves pound on the hull. Only the soft flapping of the sails marred the silence. It was almost as if they had entered a lost paradise.

She laughed in relief. "Now don't be thinking that that was high adventure. The rocks weren't as close as they looked."

"Could've fooled me," he said, and grinned at her.

She grinned back. "I must admit, you're a good man to have around in a storm."

Marnie followed the trail of silver moonlight, anxious to find her favorite anchorage before the moon disappeared altogether.

"Take the tiller, while I drop anchor," she said, then proceeded to tell him clearly and concisely what she wanted him to do.

Duke was surprised at how easily things went, and when she rejoined him in the cockpit a few minutes later, he said, "You give orders like a regular captain. Have you done it often?"

"When you're teaching a bunch of teenagers how to sail, you've got to find a way to get their attention."

"You teach kids to sail?"

"Among other things."

"Sounds interesting, and I'd like to hear more about it later," he said, then waved his hand at the boat. "Meanwhile, how can I help you stow these sails?"

They worked well together, Marnie thought again, pleased at how willingly Duke took orders. She was pleased, also, by his happy hum and the graceful way he moved and bent and stretched—as graceful as a mountain cougar. His long legs were powerful, his upper body trim, and she wondered how he stayed in such good shape when he obviously spent long hours behind a desk.

Duke stopped humming and looked up from his crouched position on the deck. "Yes, I'm liking this adventure more and more with every passing minute," he said huskily, his eyes narrowed with speculation.

Suddenly, Marnie became aware of what she had done. She had moored herself for the night next to a deserted island, with a very sexy man. And there was only one bed on the boat.

"Oh no!" Marnie exclaimed, and abruptly threw the sailbag at Duke. Startled, Duke rose to catch it, cracking his head on the boom. Marnie watched in horror as he catapulted overboard.

"Oh, dear Lord, please help," Marnie prayed as she began hauling on the safety line that attached Duke to the boat. "Please help me get him back on board."

He was unconscious, but the life jacket kept his head out of water as she pulled him up against the hull. Leaning over the gunwale, she anxiously touched his face. He was ice cold, but thankfully she could feel his warm breath against her fingers. "Duke. Duke. Wake up."

He moaned and coughed but made no answer, and she didn't waste time calling out again, because every second he spent in the water increased his chances of dying from hypothermia. She had to get him on board fast. Swinging the boom into position, she attached Duke's safety harness to the rope and began pulling on it.

His bowed head came into view, and Marnie kept hauling, wishing she had six hands so she could protect him from hitting things as she swung the boom back and brought him aboard. He hung limply, and she pushed open the hatch and carefully lowered him into the cabin.

Scrambling below, she quickly lit the kerosene lamp, then knelt beside the still-unconscious man. His lips were blue, his skin pale, and he was shivering. Marnie didn't like the looks of things, not one little bit.

Clarence bounded across the floor, licked Duke's face, and gave a loud *meow* of concern.

"I know, I know," Marnie told Clarence as she began unfastening the safety harness and life jacket. "We have to get his clothes off. Otherwise he can still die of hypothermia."

With his life jacket off, she began pulling up his sweater, grunting and groaning with the effort of lifting his body. "Zeus! He's heavier than he looks," she muttered, then sucked in a sharp breath as she gazed down at his chest. "No wonder. He's all muscle."

Rising to her feet, she stepped back into the bathroom and removed a stack of towels from beneath the sink. After wrapping one around Duke's head, she covered his chest with the others, then began tugging at his boots.

"He'll never wear these again, which is a real shame because they were beautiful. And expensive." She sighed in resignation. "So much for getting any money out of King Oil. Duke isn't going to be in a very charitable mood when he wakes up. But the main thing is to make sure he does wake up!"

She reached for the belt of his slacks, thankful that they weren't skintight jeans. But his black briefs were tight, she discovered a moment later, making her heart-stoppingly aware of his tanned, muscular thighs as she skimmed the wet cotton over them.

"Do you think he'll mind being stripped buck

naked by a stranger, Clarence?" she asked, the words catching in her throat. "And a woman at that?"

"*Meow.*"

"You're absolutely right, Clarence. Of course he'll mind. But we'll worry about that later."

Keeping her eyes averted was impossible, and Marnie draped towels over the lower half of King's body before she began gently rubbing him dry. Violent shivers racked his body, and Marnie was tempted to give him a brisk rubdown. But she resisted, aware that he needed the warmth of blood in his inner core if he was going to survive.

She was debating how she was going to get him into bed when he moaned and began pulling at the towels. She reached out to restrain him, and he caught her hands with surprising strength for a man who was still semiconscious.

"Duke. Can you hear me? Wake up," Marnie called.

His eyelids opened slightly, and he stared up at her blindly, his teeth chattering. "C-Cold. C-Cold."

"I know, but if you can stand up, we'll get you into bed."

His eyes closed, and Marnie felt his hands go slack. She squeezed them, trying to transmit some strength into him. "Don't pass out on me, Duke. I can't lift you by myself. You'll have to help me."

He opened his eyes, and she saw the war he

waged to stay awake. He had three good reasons to be unconscious: the knockout drops, the crack on his head, and the strength-sapping cold. Any normal man would still be unconscious, but not Duke King. He grunted again.

"Come on, Duke. Stand up. You can do it," she encouraged, pulling on his hands.

Without saying a word, he slowly sat up. The towels fell into his lap, and Marnie quickly secured one around his waist. When she settled his arm over her shoulder and wrapped her arm around his back, he flinched. "Damn."

"Is anything broken?" she asked, looking worriedly at his back. "The boom really clipped you a whack."

Tentatively, he rolled his shoulders and moved his arm. "Don't think so . . . hurts like the blue blazes."

"Well, you'll be completely blue if we don't get you into bed. Now use me as a leaning post. Don't be afraid to put your weight on me. I'm strong."

Using Marnie for leverage, Duke shoved himself to his feet, then clung to her, his head slumped on her shoulder, his arm braced against her breast. "Yeah. So soft . . . but so strong."

There wasn't one thing soft about Duke, Marnie thought as together they staggered toward the forward cabin. With one hand she pulled back the blankets, and after he had collapsed onto the bed, she covered him, piling on a sleeping bag for good measure. Only then did she take a moment to breathe a sigh of relief.

He had lost consciousness again and wasn't out of the woods yet, but at least he had a fighting chance. Now all she had to do was get something hot into him.

While the kettle boiled, she took his wet clothes up on deck and quickly stowed the sails. Satisfied that they'd weather the night, she returned below and pulled the hatch closed, just as rain began to fall.

The cedar planking glowed in the lamplight, and the flames beneath the kettle were already warming the salon. Under other circumstances Marnie would have been content.

But the pirate in the forecabin wouldn't be the least bit content when he woke up, Marnie surmised. And she couldn't blame him. With a sigh she began making the tea.

He must be in hell, Duke thought, and lay still, fighting to control the panic rising up inside him. Hell was hot and full of demons who had worked over his back and shoulder with sledgehammers and were now pounding holes in his skull. Worse yet, something was sitting on his chest, weighing him down.

Slowly, Duke opened his eyes . . . and met the disapproving stare of a one-eyed cat. With a *meow* of disdain, the yellow cat stood up—on three legs—then jumped off Duke and disappeared.

Fighting his way out from under the tangle of covers, Duke sat up abruptly. And cracked his head.

With a muttered oath he fell back against the pillow, just as his other bed partner bounced upright. Holy hell, a woman, he thought, and stared at her in disbelief and dismay. A cat was bad enough!

"Thank goodness you're awake," she said, gazing down at him, her sea-green eyes full of concern.

Sea-green eyes. Saucy red-gold curls that tumbled over her shoulders. And a nymphlike quality to her features, almost as if she didn't belong in this world. He'd seen her before, he knew. But where?

"How are you feeling?" she asked, reaching out to touch his face.

Her fingers felt cool against his skin, and he captured her hand, wanting to bring it to his dry, cracked lips. Instead, he moved it to his temple and wasn't the least bit surprised when the demons let up a little.

"Where did you come from?" he asked hoarsely.

"I own this boat."

"I'm on a boat?"

"Yes."

Lowering their still-clasped hands to his chest, he looked around, taking in the berth, the sloping cabin, the low-lying ceiling. "What am I doing on your boat?"

"I . . . it . . ."

He pressed her hand against his chest. "In bed with you—naked."

She glanced down at his bare chest and felt her cheeks burn as she remembered how, in fatigue and desperation, she had finally changed into sweats and climbed into the bed, snuggling close to him in an effort to warm him up. At first he had been colder than a corpse, but gradually his temperature had begun to rise. And so had hers—to the boiling point—fueled by the fact that his body had been hard and masculine and naked.

As she lay beside Duke, she had realized just how much she wanted to share her life, as well as her bed, with a man. She'd spent part of the night debating if she should say yes to Gil's proposal. The rest of the night she'd spent wondering what it would be like to share a bed with Duke when he wasn't unconscious. But he wasn't unconscious now; he was awake and demanding answers.

"Your clothes were soaked. You fell overboard," she told him, hoping he wouldn't remember why.

"So you rescued me all by yourself, put me to bed, and then climbed in to comfort me."

"You were freezing cold!"

"I'm no longer freezing, so you must have done a good job of warming me up." He studied her thoughtfully, wishing he could recall more about the previous night. Why did he have such a hell of a hangover? Why was he in bed with a beautiful woman? At least he had finally remembered her name. "So tell me, Marnie MacBride, how a tiny little sprite like you managed to pull me out of the water."

"It's a long story. I'll make some coffee, then fill you in on the details." She attempted to pull her hand away, but he refused to let it go.

"All the details?"

"Yes."

"You kissed me, didn't you, Marnie? In this bed."

She looked down at him, remembering how she had kissed him to keep him quiet, and knowing what she had felt for him then was skin-deep compared to what she would feel if he were to kiss her now. For now he was sober and in control and looking handsomer than any man had a right to look, with his tousled hair, his twenty-four-hour beard, and his sexy, hair-matted chest.

"Yes, I kissed you," she whispered.

He nodded. "But nothing else happened."

"How can you be so certain of that?"

"Because if we had made love, you wouldn't be wearing clothes, and you wouldn't be looking at me with so much speculation in your eyes."

She felt her cheeks flush again, and she suspected it would be a normal occurrence if she spent any time around Duke King. He had a way of looking at her that made her feel like molten lava sitting on the lip of a volcano. "Oh, so you're quite the lover boy, are you?" she asked.

"So I've been told." Then, giving up the Don Juan pretense, he grimaced. "And I wouldn't mind proving it to you, except my mouth tastes like a barefoot army has marched through it, and my head feels as if it were still drumming the beat."

She laughed softly, delighted to see that Duke still retained his sense of humor . . . even though it was well disguised. "If you'll let me go, I'll see if I can come up with a maritimer's remedy for what ails you," she said.

He glanced down at his chest, surprised to see that he was still holding her hand, and reluctantly released it.

After she left the cabin, Duke lay with his arm bent, his wrist over his eyes, collecting his senses. Yes, he was on a boat. He could hear the waves slapping on the hull, smell the salt air. And somewhere in the distance a horn sounded, deep and forlorn and eerie. He didn't have the strength to raise his head and look out the porthole to confirm whether or not it was foggy outside.

Instead, he raised his arm and peered at his wristwatch—the only thing that had apparently survived his dip in the sea. Damn! He had to chair a meeting in two hours. He'd better get going.

He had managed to lever himself into a semi-sitting position when Marnie slid back the door and handed him a terry-cloth robe and a pair of wool socks. "Last night's rain washed the salt out of your clothes, but they'll take most of the day to dry," she explained. "Sorry, this is all I can find for you to wear. They won't fit, so wrap a blanket around yourself for extra warmth. And if you want to use the facilities, the head is at the stern—or the back of the boat, to you landlubbers."

Duke managed a tight grin at the idiosyncrasies of the English language, but the smile faded entirely as he pulled on the robe. Who in hell did it fit, he wondered, a midget? It barely covered him, reaching midthigh. No, make that upper thigh, he discovered moments later when he bent over to pull on the socks. The demons began pounding in his head again, and he gave up on the socks.

He ignored Marnie completely as he stumbled through the salon into the head. Taking a deep breath, he shut the door and told himself that there was lots of room, lots of breathing space. And he didn't have to spend more than two minutes in these cramped quarters. Two minutes. He could hold his breath for much longer than two minutes, if necessary.

The thermos held just enough hot water to wash his face and hands and remind him of how salty and itchy the rest of his body felt. He'd give his right arm to be at home in his large bathroom, taking a long hot shower, about now. But he wasn't even going to get a short cold shower, he realized as he took a quick glance around the bathroom. It was beautifully paneled in cedar and contained a john and a sink, but no shower.

Well, it didn't really matter, he decided as the walls began to close in on him. He'd only be able to stay there long enough to brush his teeth with the new toothbrush Marnie had provided. His teeth felt better, but that was the extent of his well-being as he slid open the door and stepped into the salon.

Marnie turned away from the gimbaled stove to smile at him, looking so soft and feminine in her faded blue jeans and sweater of muted blues, greens, and mauves. Looking so regal with her chin tilted just so, like a goddess.

"Sorry I can't offer you a chair," she said, "but you have a choice of the floor or the companionway, if you want to sit down."

He glanced around the salon, really seeing it for the first time. Except for the galley, it was completely gutted down to the beautiful white-oak ribs and yellow-cedar planking.

Cushions from the bed were piled on the floor against the bulkhead of the forward cabin, but the floor was a long way down, and getting there would be too dangerous in his state of dress—or rather, undress.

His clothes, he noted in disgust, were strung out on a line, dripping into a plastic bucket.

"I've heard about bare-bones charter outfits, but this is the barest boat I've ever seen."

She flashed him an apologetic smile. "I'm restoring it in my spare time."

"And what else do you do in your spare time?"

"Concoct hangover remedies." She handed him a steaming mug. "I think you had better sit down while you drink it."

He took it, sniffing it suspiciously while he eased his butt onto the middle step of the companionway and braced his legs to hold himself there. "I don't have a hangover."

"You could've fooled me." He was looking remarkably sexy, Marnie thought, despite his bleary eyes and his furrowed forehead. And it wasn't simply the short robe he was wearing, either. There was something about him that made her breath catch in her throat and her insides tie into a knot every time she looked at him. She had hoped she'd be able to control her reactions when they were both out of bed, but she had underestimated the devastating effect he had on her.

"I never get drunk," he muttered.

"So you told me while you were swinging on the mast. But I wager you don't make a habit of drinking Mickey Finns, either. Drink the concoction—it's guaranteed to cure what ails you."

"What is it?"

"Witches' brew."

He sipped cautiously. "It tastes like it."

"When you're finished, I'll give you some aspirin with your coffee. Meanwhile, aren't you going to put on those socks?"

"It would be suicide to bend over in my condition. Would you like to put them on for me?"

She took one look at the length of bare, muscular leg that stretched out from beneath his robe and quickly averted her gaze, knowing her ears were burning. "No way."

"I thought not." He sipped the brew slowly, and with each mouthful he felt a bit better. However, he wasn't ready to tackle his socks or to do what he really wanted—pull back the hatch and step out into the fresh air. The cabin was spacious, but it still threatened to close in on him.

"Lord, but I'll be good and ready to get off this boat," he muttered after he drained the mug. "I get claustrophobic in cramped quarters."

"Oh dear," Marnie said, extending her hand for his mug. "I'm afraid you won't be getting off as soon as you had hoped."

"What do you mean by that?" he asked, his eyes narrowing as he saw the guilty expression on her face. "What the devil is going on here?"

Refusing to be intimidated by his stern voice and forbidding features, Marnie took her time about rinsing the mug and refilling it with coffee. She handed it to him, along with the promised aspirin, then leaned back against the counter and folded her arms across her chest.

"Okay, I'll tell you what is going on," she said sweetly. "You, Mister In-control King, pulled a real boner last night. You walked into a pub alone, certain you were invincible. You knew the protesters were there and that they were angry, and you should have stayed in the resort with the rest of the oilmen who were attending the conference. But no, you had to go out and beard the lions in their den."

"I thought I could talk to them, tell them about the safeguards we intend to put in place. In fact, I was making some progress when I suddenly felt the room go around."

"The Mickey Finn. While you were talking, three hotheads were busy ambushing you with knockout drops in your drink, and planning to do other dire things to you."

"And what were you doing in the pub?"

The skeptical look in his granite-gray eyes would have given his strongest opponent second thoughts, and Marnie drew in a shaky breath before answering honestly, "Following you."

"Were you after my money or my bod?"

"Why would you think that I'd want either?" Marnie asked in surprise.

He looked at her over the rim of his coffee cup. "Because that's all women seem to want from me."

"No wonder you're as approachable as a wounded sea lion."

"So you've learned that about me already? Good for you."

She'd learned a lot more—such as how warm and humorous he was—but she didn't think he would be in the mood to hear about that discovery. "I got the message loud and clear," she said softly, and turned her back to dish up breakfast. "That's why I decided it was no use hanging around and went back to my boat. Then you came staggering down to the marina with the men on your tail. After weighing all the options, I decided it was safest to get you out of there."

He looked at the plate of scrambled eggs and toast she handed him and decided it might be safe to taste it. Slowly, he tried a mouthful, and when his stomach didn't revolt, he ate another. "So you shanghaied me on board and sailed off with me, all because you thought you had to rescue me?"

"Something like that."

"I did not need rescuing," he stated emphatically, pointing the fork at her to make his point.

She swallowed a piece of toast and smiled smugly. "So you say."

Duke looked at Marnie, wondering why this slight slip of a woman was standing up to him. Normally, he could intimidate the backbone out of any opponent with a cold look or a few caustic words. Neither seemed to have any effect on Marnie. "Why didn't you call out for help?" he asked, handing her his empty plate.

She took it, offered seconds, and, when he refused, refilled his mug. "There was no one else around," she said, answering his question. "The boats in the marina belong to summer tourists who fly in to the resort for a holiday. And the lodge was too far away for anyone to hear me."

She turned away and began cleaning the dishes,

and he studied her in silence, trying to remember what had happened the previous evening. Slowly, it returned, the smell of lavender, the taste of her lips as he'd kissed her . . . a few words.

"You really did come to kidnap me, didn't you?" he asked harshly, suspicion congealing into a queasy lump in the pit of his stomach.

She swung around and saw the distrust in his eyes; hers darkened with dismay. "What are you talking about?"

"I remember lying in that bed fighting the effects of that Mickey Finn, and I heard you call out that you were leaving because you had gotten what you had come for. Me."

"That's not true. I came to see you, all right, but not to get you."

"How did you know I was going to be at the resort? The meeting was top secret."

"Top secret! Who are you kidding? Everyone on the islands knew the oilmen were going to hold a conference at the resort."

"So we learned when the protesters crashed the meeting." His eyes grew colder, bleaker. "You were there, too, acting as a helper, weren't you? How did you manage that?"

"The owner was returning a favor."

"Makes me wonder whether he was in on it too."

"Oh, for heaven's sake! All I wanted was an opportunity to talk to you." She pushed her hair off her forehead with an impatient hand. "Not you specifically. Any CEO would have met my needs." That was what she had told herself before she had arrived at the meeting. One glimpse of Mr. Duke King, however, and she had decided that he was the only man she could approach. Because cold gray eyes notwithstanding, he was the only man she felt would listen to her. Would give her a chance. But he had been too involved with the protesters even to look at her. And now it was too late.

"You mean you would've kidnapped Sanders or Nash or one of the other guys?" Duke asked.

She sighed in exasperation. "How many times do I have to tell you that I did not kidnap you?"

"Then take me back. I have to chair the conference this morning." He glanced pointedly at his watch. "And it starts in seventy-three minutes."

"I know, and believe me, the only reason I brought you aboard was so you could attend the conference in one piece. I was going to hire a float-plane to fly you back this morning."

"So?"

"So the storm came up. Remember? And we had to put in here to find safe harbor."

"It isn't storming now."

"Now it's foggy."

"What does fog have to do with it?"

"Fog means I can't see more than two feet in front of the boat. And it also means there's no wind."

This time he raised one elegantly arched black eyebrow and waited.

"And . . . and I don't have an engine," she finally admitted, hardly daring to look at him.

He threw up his hands in disbelief, then quickly lowered them to pull his robe back in place. "Whoever heard of going out on the ocean without an engine?"

"I'm a purist," she said, trying to keep from grinning at his predicament but failing.

"Pure, my foot. You are a conniving witch. You want something from me, and you think this is a surefire way to get it." He glared at her. "Lady, you're walking a fine edge. I've never done bodily harm to a woman in my life, but there is always a first time."

Unperturbed by his Captain Ahab expression, she continued to smile. "You would never harm me."

"How can you be so sure?"

"Because I put my life in your hands last night, and you kept me safe," she said softly.

Suddenly, he felt rotten about the way he'd been acting toward her. "You're right." He rubbed his hand over his face and smiled at her sheepishly. "Could we row ashore and find someone with a boat to take me back?"

He looked so sick, so tired, that it was all Marnie could do not to reach out and pull his head against her breast and soothe his temples. "I'm sorry,

Duke. The island is a marine park. No one lives there, and no one will be around, especially in the winter."

"So radio for help."

"I was afraid you would think of that." She sighed. "I can't. I haven't installed my radio yet."

"What! You went sailing with no engine, no radio, with a storm on the way?"

"The storm wasn't suppose to arrive until tomorrow, but I guess Venus decided to get into the act."

"Venus? What's a Greek goddess got to do with it?"

"Ah . . . well . . ." she said, regretting her previous statement. Besides, it wasn't Venus's fault she was stranded in the fog with a handsome man, was it? And it wasn't Venus's fault that Duke could do more to excite her by looking at her than Gil could with his most passionate kiss—although if she counted the number of times both men had kissed her, they would be pretty much on a par. Their kisses, however, were definitely not on a par.

Duke raised a skeptical eyebrow. "You believe in gods?"

"Not really." She wiggled her nose, then gave him a hesitant smile. "Well, maybe I do—at least a little. I believe in lots of different things, you see. It makes life much more interesting."

His look of disbelief changed to one of speculation. "If I remember my Greek mythology correctly, Venus was the goddess of love?"

"Ah, yes," Marnie said, backing up against the counter, definitely wishing she hadn't brought up the subject. "She was also the goddess of the sea."

With one lithe movement he was standing in front of her, invading the small galley with his masculine presence. Startled, she pressed her hands to her breast.

He gazed at her, remembering the storm, remembering how she had ridden the boat, looking as if she had risen from the sea. "You're the goddess of the sea," he said softly. "You're Venus."

She tried to say something, but the words wouldn't form in her brain, much less pass through her tight throat. Planting both hands on the cupboard, one on each side of her head, he leaned forward and continued, "So it might be much more interesting to forget about the conference and use my time to learn about love."

"I'm sure a man like you already knows all he needs to know about love," she whispered, wondering if he knew how close she was to melting into a pool of saltwater toffee at his feet.

"I know about lies and deceit. Not love."

"You think I'm lying to you?" she asked, her voice squeaking in indignation.

"What else should I think?"

"That I have been telling the truth because I always tell the truth." Placing her hands on his chest, she pushed, and when he moved back slightly, she sucked in a grateful breath. "And while we're at it, let's get one more thing straight. I know your head is aching and you're feeling lousy, so I'll forgive your bad temper." She tapped his chest again, her traitorous fingers lingering on his warm flesh a moment before she snatched her hands away. "However, you are going to have a hot scrub-down and a nap. And when you get up, you are going to be a civil human being, or I'll throw you overboard and let the sharks eat you. Did you get that?"

"I got it, all right, and you frighten me, except for one thing." He gave her a wicked smile, then stepped aside. "The only shark in these waters is on board this boat."

THREE

"Are my clothes dry?" Duke asked hopefully as he entered the salon a few hours later.

"I'm afraid they won't be dry until morning," Marnie said, glancing up from the Turk's head knots she was fashioning into a coaster to smile at him. The smile faded, and her eyes widened as they took in Duke's apparel. He had wrapped a white sheet around his waist and draped the end over his shoulder, Roman-toga style. His legs were long, and the skirt was short . . . and she remembered all too vividly what lay under it. "That is, if I don't dunk them overboard again," she dared to tease him as she rose from the companionway and stepped into the galley.

Not for all the oil in Texas was he going to let Marnie guess how foolish he felt, Duke decided as he turned around in a slow circle. "You like?"

He looked so outrageously masculine that even her tummy quivered in admiration. "I love. The Roman period suits you."

"If I'm going to have a grand adventure, I might as well look the part," Duke said. With a flourish he sank onto the pile of cushions and propped himself up on one elbow.

Laughing softly, Marnie brought him a mug of coffee, kneeling to hand it to him. He took it, and she patted his wrist, her fingers lingering against his hair-roughened skin.

He smiled at her, a boyish smile that must have won the heart of every girl he'd ever met, Marnie thought, as she slowly drew away from him and settled on a pillow. But now the smile was a bit cynical, and a whole lot sensual, and the combination was devastating.

"Thanks for being such a good sport," she said, casually folding her arms around her bent knees.

Duke nodded and took a sip of coffee. "And thanks for the coffee. It sure hits the spot." He swallowed again and looked at her over the brim of the mug. "I guess there isn't any hope that we'll be leaving soon?"

"None. The fog is thicker than it was this morning."

"How long do you think it's going to last?"

"A day, maybe two."

She had spent most of the day alternately fussing at and feeling thankful for the fog. One minute she wanted this dangerous, sexy man out of her life as soon as possible, and the next minute she wanted him to stay so she could get to know him better. And now she was so confused, she didn't really know what she wanted.

"Isn't there anyone who will be worried about you?" he asked, staring at her in concern.

"Mom and Dad are in San Francisco attending the opening of Mom's show—she's a sculptor, you see—and the boatyard is closed for the holiday. I have to cook Thanksgiving dinner, but this is only Monday. We should be home by then." She frowned, trying to remember something very important about Thanksgiving that kept escaping her. "And thank goodness Desiree is feeding the orphans for me."

"Orphans?"

"Not children. Birds and animals."

"I see," Duke said, looking at the big yellow cat that was sitting on the top step of the companionway, washing his face with his only front paw. "Is that one of your orphans?"

Marnie half turned her head, caught sight of the cat, and smiled, then looked back at Duke. "Clarence? Yes, I did take him in after he lost his leg. His owner didn't want him any longer."

"So you make a habit of rescuing animals, do you?"

"Mmm."

"And people?"

He was staring at her with such a funny expression on his face that Marnie felt the blood rush to her cheeks. She chewed her bottom lip. "I'm sorry I couldn't get you back in time for the conference."

"I imagine they'll manage without me."

"But they'll be worried about your disappearance. Oh, I wish I hadn't acted so impulsively. Maybe I should have tried harder to bluff my way out of it. But Booring had a gun, and I had visions of him killing you and . . ."

Reaching out, Duke patted her shoulder, but when he started to withdraw his hand, his fingers became tangled in her hair. "It's okay, sea witch," he said as he absently toyed with her curls.

She held her breath, wondering why his mere touch was enough to make her scalp tingle in anticipation. Wondering how it would feel if he, once again, caressed more than her hair. The thought rattled her, and she rushed into speech. "I do it all the time, you know. Get into trouble, I mean, because I'm off in my make-believe world. Dad says it will be the death of me yet."

He laughed hoarsely. "Oh, Marnie, Marnie, you're so good for me."

"I know. I make you laugh." She laughed with him, and their gazes met and held fast as they shared the moment.

His eyes were alive with quicksilver, Marnie noted, and the warmth in them made more than her scalp tingle. Her eyes were flashing like emeralds,

Duke thought, and wondered when he had last been so vitally aware of a woman. Gradually, they stopped laughing. Gradually, he removed his fingers from her hair.

"You should laugh more often," she said gently. "It's good for what ails you."

"I haven't had much to laugh about these past few years," he said, his fleeting feeling of happiness disappearing even as he spoke. He shut his eyes, counting, remembering. "Four years and forty-one days to be exact."

He opened his eyes, and Marnie saw the raw pain in their depths before they became cold again. "That's a long time to be unhappy," she said softly, wondering who or what had hurt him, and whether she could help. Instantly, she pushed the thought aside. Mr. Duke King would neither want nor appreciate her butting into his affairs.

She rose to her feet, but not before Duke saw the sympathetic look she gave him. It shook him, touched something deep inside him, and he watched in silence as she moved back to the companionway and picked up the string she'd been working with. Why would a perfect stranger be worrying about him? he wondered. And why was he responding to her warmth?

He thought of the years that stretched ahead of him. Long, empty, lonely years. Lord, it was tempting to take what happiness he could, right there, right now, with this lovely, warmhearted woman.

But as much as he was tempted, he couldn't take what she might possibly offer him. Marnie deserved more than a one-night stand, and that was all he could give her in return.

"So what would you like to do for the rest of the evening?" Marnie asked, turning from the sink to look at Duke, who was lounging on the cushions. She had refused his offer of assistance with the dishes, out of self-preservation. The galley wasn't big enough to hold both of them—and her overactive imagination!

Take you to bed and make love with you. The words popped into Duke's mind, giving substance to the thoughts that had been nibbling on the edge during dinner. He knew he shouldn't be thinking them, but that didn't stop him from savoring the idea of removing her clothes and exploring her beautiful body with his lips and hands. And then making slow, sweet love to her.

"You wouldn't happen to have a pack of cards on this boat, would you?" he asked as he leaned back on the cushion propped up against the bulkhead.

She bent to open one of the bottom drawers. "It just so happens I do."

"Now why doesn't that surprise me?" he asked with a chuckle, admiring the way her soft, faded jeans fit her saucy backside. "You've already produced a steak dinner—"

"Compliments of the Raynaird Resort in lieu of payment for services rendered." Crossing the floor, she sank onto her cushion, then placed the cards, two tumblers, and a bottle on the floor beside her.

"And now out comes the scotch."

"In my family you can't play cards without scotch." She splashed the amber liquor into the tumblers and handed him one, then brushed a wayward lock of hair off her cheek with her fingers.

Duke watched in silent appreciation as her snug sweater tugged and stretched against her firm, rounded breasts. "Here I thought you were going to ply me with liquor and seduce me," he said, thinking that it wouldn't take much effort on her part.

Marnie had to admit that the thought had crossed her mind a time or two during dinner. It wasn't easy to forget how she'd felt when Duke had kissed her, and it was totally impossible to ignore how handsome and masculine he looked—despite the fact that he was still wearing the sheet. His thick black hair fell rakishly over his forehead, and his black two-day beard made him look piratical. No, he wasn't a pirate, she decided, his features were too aristocratic. He was a god. All that he needed was a bowl of olives and a couple of goddesses in flowing veils to complete the bedchamber scene.

"Me, seduce you?" she asked huskily, trying not to look past his heart-stopping knees. "I'm not the one wearing the skirt."

"I'll remember that remark, sea witch," he warned, but spoiled the effect with another chuckle. "Meanwhile, name your game."

"Poker."

"Strip?"

She eyed his apparel as she picked up the cards. "It would be over in one hand."

"You cheat?"

"Who? Me? Never." She shuffled the cards with a satisfying ripple. "But have you ever heard of Tom O'Shaughnessy? He taught me everything I know."

He had never heard of O'Shaughnessy, and he half-suspected that no one else had ever heard of him, either. Marnie, he was discovering to his delight, had a vivid imagination and seemed to live in a make-believe world full of gods and larger-than-life people. "It sounds as if you'll take me for everything I own," he said, giving her a wry smile, "but name the stakes."

She sipped her scotch as she considered the options and finally came up with one that suited her fancy. "The person who loses has to answer the question the winner asks."

"Honestly?"

"That's the only way to answer a question, isn't it?"

"Yeah. So you'll be asking me what my favorite color is. Right?"

She smiled serenely, dealt, played the hand, and laid down three kings to beat his two jacks.

"You do cheat!" he said, as he raised his glass and took his first drink of scotch.

"So what do you want to be when you grow up?" she asked, wiggling into a more comfortable position on her cushion.

Her wiggle rocked the boat slightly, but it rocked Duke a hell of a lot more. He took a deep breath, willing his blood to simmer down. Willing his loins to stop aching for her.

"What happened to 'What's your favorite color?'" he asked, his voice as mellow as the scotch.

"Answer the question, Duke."

He shrugged. "Run King Oil."

"That's what you're doing now. What do you really want to be?"

This time he considered his answer, and this time his voice was dead serious as he spoke. "All I've ever wanted to *do* was run King Oil. All I've ever wanted to *be* was the president of King Oil. Unfortunately, my father is still throwing his weight around, even though he had a stroke this summer. Don't get me wrong. I don't want him dead, by any means. I just wish he would officially turn the reins over to me and get the hell out of my hair."

"It sounds as if you've had problems with him."

"A few. The Baron isn't a businessman, and he's—" Duke frowned at his drink, then set it down on the floor, wondering why one sip had loosened his tongue. He had never before said those words, not even to his father, and here he was spilling his guts to this lovely redheaded lady. If he wasn't careful, it was going to be a very revealing evening.

"Last night you told me all you ever do is work," Marnie said thoughtfully. "Wouldn't being the president of King Oil mean you'd have to work even longer hours?"

"If I didn't have to worry about the Baron screwing things up every time I left, I could delegate more of my responsibilities, take more time off."

"So when are you going to settle it?"

Duke looked at Marnie, trying to decide if she really was a witch. How else could she have guessed that he had been wrestling with that question for the last four months? "I don't know. The man is so damn proud, and now that he's had the stroke, it's even harder to knock the pins out from under him. I'm not sure he would survive if he didn't have King Oil, but . . ."

Marnie nodded in understanding. "What does your mother have to say about all this?"

"Madre supports the Baron; she always has, but she worries about him too. The Duchess, my grandmother, keeps giving me broad hints that the Baron might be distracted by a grandson."

"Then why don't you provide him with one?" Marnie teased, and was surprised by the flash of pain that filled his eyes. It was gone immediately, replaced by the somber gray of a cloud-covered sea.

"That isn't in the cards," he said harshly, looking down at his hands, wishing suddenly that he was wearing his Stetson. His gaze sought its resting place on the counter, then returned reluctantly to Marnie's face. "Speaking of cards, I thought the stakes were limited to one question. Deal."

"So are you married?" she asked when she won the next hand. The question was long overdue, especially since she'd spent the day dreaming about him.

"I watched you like a hawk, and I didn't see you cheating."

"Lucky thing we aren't playing strip poker, isn't it? You'd be naked by now."

Realizing what she had said, Marnie wiggled in embarrassment, and warm blood heated her cheeks.

Blood rushed to her cheeks about as fast as it rushed to his loins, Duke thought in wry amusement, and wondered whether she blushed all over. And if he would ever discover that fact for himself.

"Maybe that was what I had in mind," he said, his voice low and husky.

She pressed the cool cards against her cheeks, trying to relieve the heat.

"The question was . . ." she whispered.

He continued to gaze at her for a few more seconds, admiring the way the lamplight spun webs of gold in her tumble of red curls, then took pity on her. "I know what the question was, and the answer is no."

Slowly, she lowered her hands, keeping her gaze

riveted on her fingers as they toyed with the cards. "Funny. I could have sworn you were married."

"Why?"

"Well, a man as good-looking as you are should've been married by now." She raised her gaze to meet his. "You're what, forty?"

"Thirty-six, and I'm not gay. I was married once, for six years." He shrugged a bare, elegant shoulder. "Good old Cupid managed to hit me with one of his poisonous arrows, but it didn't last."

"You're divorced?"

"Yeah. I came home from a three-month business trip, and Karen informed me that she wanted a divorce so she could marry one of my best friends." She had also told him something else—something he'd vowed to take silently to his grave.

"Oh, Duke. How awful for you." Without thinking, Marnie reached out and touched Duke's bare knee. One feel of his hard, warm flesh, however, and she jerked her hand away.

Duke looked at Marnie, amused by her fluster but warmed by her concern. Never once had Karen reached out to comfort him. But then, Karen had had needs that he had never met. "It wasn't all Karen's fault," Duke said quietly. "I wasn't great husband material. I was away a lot and worked long hours when I was at home, so I couldn't spend as much time with her as she wanted."

"Are you going to get married again?" she asked, thinking that his wife had been very foolish. If this man were her husband, she would never let him go.

"No. Never."

The two words were stark, uncompromising, making Marnie want to shake him, to urge him not to give up so easily. "Why not?" she asked instead.

"Because I don't believe in love. Even if I did, I'll never trust another woman enough to marry her. Besides, I—" He took another swallow of scotch, then waggled the tumbler at her. "And that's three questions. Deal."

The cards were definitely going her way tonight, Marnie thought as she laid down another winning hand a few minutes later. Although she was still stewing about what Duke had told her, she couldn't help a triumphant grin as she looked up at him. "Why are you claustrophobic?"

"Marnie, when are you going to ask an easy question?"

"That's no fun."

"Just wait till I get a turn," he warned. "If you ever stop cheating, that is."

She continued to grin as she waited for his answer.

"When I was five, I was kidnapped and held for ransom."

Her grin faded, replaced by a look of dismay. "Oh, Duke! I'm so sorry. I shouldn't have teased about kidnapping you."

"It's all right, Marnie," he assured her quickly. "You couldn't have known."

"Tell me what happened, please," she said, her eyes brimming with sudden tears she couldn't stop.

Dumbfounded by her tears, he shook his head and found himself wanting to lean over and kiss them away. Instead, he settled his shoulders deeper into the cushion.

"The man held me in a small root cellar on an old, abandoned farm," he said quietly. "Afterward, I learned that it was two weeks before my grandfather and father could scrape up the money for the ransom. Something went wrong at the drop, and the kidnapper was killed. It was another three days before they found me."

She gasped. "You were all alone in the dark? What did you do?"

"I sang." He laughed briefly, trying to lighten the mood. "Mom had always told us that if we were frightened, we should whistle. I couldn't whistle, but I could sing. My grandmother sang, and she taught me almost as soon as I could talk. That's how they found me. Someone was out riding and heard me singing."

"You must have been so frightened," she said, absently dabbing at the tears with her sleeve.

"And hungry, and so happy to see my family. It took me a long time before I could go to sleep without a light in the room. And I still have trouble riding elevators."

"Your poor mother must have been sick with worry."

Duke smiled tenderly, thinking how kindhearted Marnie was. She had instinctively homed in on how he had felt, then how his mother had felt. Marnie's concern, her caring manner, warmed him somehow . . . made him feel good. "It was years before Madre would let my brothers and me out of sight without a bodyguard," he admitted softly, "and that was only after we had become firearms and judo experts."

"But you still, to this day, keep an eye on the other two, don't you?"

"That goes with the territory of being the oldest."

"No wonder you're so serious. The whole experience has left a mark on you."

"Yeah. I hate small places."

"And you don't sing anymore." When he raised a questioning eyebrow, she explained, "Last night, when you were serenading me, you said you didn't sing anymore."

He rubbed his chin thoughtfully. "The kidnapping wasn't responsible for that. In fact, I did a lot of singing when I was growing up—in church choirs, musicals at college, barbershop groups afterward."

"Then why did you stop?"

"Because Karen didn't want me spending what little free time I had with the boys."

Surely, they could have worked it out? Karen must have been one very spoiled lady, Marnie thought angrily. "How long has it been since your divorce?" she asked, determined not to let her anger get in the way of what was really important.

"Four years."

"My question still stands. Why don't you sing anymore?"

He stared at her, unable to come up with a good reason. The little witch was doing it to him again. Making him examine his life. Making him realize how empty it was, and that it was mostly his own fault. "And why am I letting you ask so many questions?"

The pain was in his eyes once more, making Marnie want to reach out and comfort him. But she didn't think he would even admit to the pain, much less let her comfort him. Hold it, she told herself sternly. She wasn't going to get mixed up with a man who needed her. Remember.

"I know. I know. Deal," she muttered, lowering her gaze.

"Finally, I win!" he said, laying down the next hand. He glanced up, noticed that she wouldn't quite meet his eyes, and wondered if she had cheated so he could win a hand. The little minx, he thought, and laughed softly. "Hmmm. Now what am I going to ask?" He paused until she looked at him, then put on a very sober, businesslike expression. "What would you say are your three best qualities and three worst qualities?"

She gave a hoot of laughter. "What is this? A job interview? Can't you do any better than that?"

"Give me a chance to warm up."

"Three good qualities." She gave a little wiggle as she flashed him a smile. "That's easy. I'm loyal to my friends. I love people, especially children. And I'm honest to a fault."

"I'll remember that," he said, thinking that if he were honest, he'd tell her exactly what her wiggle was doing to him, and what he would like to do about it.

"Now three bad qualities." She tapped a finger against her even white teeth. "Let me see. I talk too much. I have a temper to go with my red hair. And I need to be needed—but I'm trying to do better."

He laughed, shaking his head. "Don't change, Marnie. Don't spoil a good thing."

His words sent a warm glow of delight through her, distracting her so even though she won the next hand, all she could think to ask was, "Is Duke your real name?"

"Hey, what happened to the tough question?"

She smiled at him. "I thought I'd go easy on you for once," she said, reaching out to touch his knee briefly before picking up the cards.

Her words were innocent, her smile was innocent, and her hand was also innocent. There was no reason for him to be feeling this overwhelming flood of desire, Duke told himself. He continued to stare at her, trying to control his thoughts, trying to get a grip on his feelings, trying to remember her question.

"It's David," he said finally. "We have a tradition in our family that the oldest son of the oldest son is called David. However, my grandmother sang for royalty and started calling her husband 'King.' My father eventually became the Baron, and when I was born, they tagged me with Duke."

"I prefer David, myself. Or Davie." She considered the name, then nodded. "I think I'll call you Davie."

"Davie! That's too soft for me."

"You're right, Davie is too soft for you. David, then. But still you do have a soft side, Duke. A very soft side."

"Hmmph." And because he was feeling softer than he wanted to in his head, and harder than he wanted to in his loins, he blurted out, "Our name goes back to heraldry in England. I went over there the summer I graduated from college and did some research on our roots . . . and came home with a family tree a mile long and our coat of arms. And then I went and designed a company flag."

Marnie smiled, thinking of the tartans that decorated her parents' home and of the summer she had spent in Scotland collecting them. "Do you still have all the genealogical information?"

"No, I gave it to my brother Dare."

"Why in heaven's name would you do that?"

Because his dream would never come true, Duke answered silently. He would play along with Marnie's game, but only so far. After all, the Kings were known far and wide for one thing—their pride.

"Dare is always giving everyone else presents," Duke said indifferently. "I thought he deserved one in return."

Marnie carefully searched Duke's eyes, noting the desolation he couldn't quite hide, and decided to leave it alone—for now. Deliberately, she lost the next hand, and the look Duke gave her told her that he knew exactly what she had done. He slowly sipped his scotch, and for a moment she was afraid he was going to call it quits.

"What is your dream?" he asked finally.

"I want to teach street kids how to sail," she answered quickly.

"What!"

"I've just finished restoring another boat I can use, and I've lined up a program with the courts in Seattle. They're going to let me take a bunch of first-time offenders on board. Learning to sail the *Homeward Bound* is incidental. The main purpose of the program is to teach the kids how to work together, teach them self-reliance, help them establish their own self-worth."

"It sounds like a very worthwhile cause," he said, intrigued by her enthusiasm.

"I was hoping you would say that, because I came to the conference to try to get you, or someone from one of the other oil companies, to sponsor the program. I figured you might be handing out conscience money, so I thought I'd try and get a share. The boat is expensive to maintain, and the program needs ongoing funding for provisions and supplies. The state might kick in some bucks once it gets established, but right now they're taking a wait-and-see attitude."

So she had been after his money, Duke mused, but not for herself. The knowledge created a warm feeling near his heart, and because the feeling was so foreign, he stomped it, hard. "And that's a sensible attitude. One I plan to follow. My deal," he said, shuffling the cards.

Disappointment clouded Marnie's face, making him feel like a heel, and he was caught off guard when she lost again.

"Is there a special man in your life?" he asked abruptly.

"You sure are getting the hang of asking these questions." She gave him a half-smile. "And I'm sure you've been cheating too."

"Ah, ah. Stop procrastinating now." He wagged a finger at her. "Remember, you're honest to a fault."

"There was a man," she said slowly. "Jack. He was my high school sweetheart. Actually, he was kind of an outcast. No one thought he would amount to anything, and I kind of took him under my wing. He graduated, went on to M.I.T. and NASA, and is scheduled to go into space soon. We were engaged for years, and I kept hoping that we would get married but . . ."

"What happened?" Duke asked, reaching out to take her hand. When she remained silent, he turned it over and examined it, noting the long scar on the palm and the almost-healed cut on her thumb—signs that she worked with her hands.

She smiled at him, silently thanking him for his sympathy. "Two years ago Jack came home on leave and told me not to wait any longer. He was never coming back to the islands, he said. They were too slow for him. When I offered to go to Houston with him, he told me I was too slow for him as well."

"The man has rocks in his head, and he's in our space program! No wonder they're in trouble."

She laughed, then sighed, then gently removed her hand from Duke's. Her love for Jack hadn't been the passionate, all-consuming love that should be present between a man and a woman, Marnie now realized. Otherwise she wouldn't have stood on the sidelines all these years; she would've demanded to be part of Jack's life. And if he had felt that kind of love, he wouldn't have left her behind.

"My only regret is that I wasted so many years waiting for Jack," she said honestly. "I'm thirty, and the islands aren't exactly overflowing with eligible men."

"But you've found one?" he guessed.

She looked at him in surprise. "I'm not sure," she admitted after a moment, and admitted silently that her doubts had increased a hundredfold since meeting Duke. "Gil Green, my father's foreman, has asked me to marry him."

"Then why don't you?"

"It's very tempting. His wife died a couple of years ago, and he has two adorable girls who need a mother. I've always wanted children, lots of children."

Yes, Marnie would want children, Duke thought, and felt a moment of regret for what might have been.

"So, the question is the same," Duke persisted, needing an answer that would put her strictly off-limits. "Why don't you marry Gil?"

Because she didn't feel passionate about Gil, either, Marnie acknowledged to herself as suddenly everything became clear. "Because he needs me," she told Duke quietly. "He needs me for himself, needs me for his children. But he doesn't love me." She took a deep breath, coming to the decision she'd been struggling with for the past week. "I can't marry a man just because he needs me. I want him to love me too."

"The man is a fool if he doesn't love you," Duke said, gazing at her tenderly. "Maybe he hasn't told you so yet, but I'd bet my last oil well he'll tell you soon. Then you can have everything you've dreamed of—a man who loves you, children. . . ."

But that wasn't enough, Marnie thought as she shuffled the cards. "I won't be marrying Gil," she said, handing him the deck. "Deal. You've already asked more than three questions."

Caught up in the battle that waged inside, Duke absently dealt the cards and played the hand. All evening he had been wanting Marnie—even though he had kept telling himself that she was strictly off-limits. Now that he knew her hopes and hurts and dreams, he definitely couldn't have a casual fling with her. And he couldn't walk away, either. He was stuck on this damn boat!

"I win," Marnie said, then repeated it once more. When she had captured his attention, she smiled and asked, "In the last six months, what has been the most significant event in your life?"

"You kidnapped me," he said, attempting to reestablish the easygoing atmosphere that had been present during the earlier part of the evening.

"Besides that."

"Nothing has even come close to the experience of meeting you."

"I'm sure you can think of something," she said, tilting the glass so the last drops of scotch would run onto her tongue.

He frowned, trying to give her question some serious thought while he watched her tongue move around the rim of the glass. "I guess it would be this summer, when I stood looking down at my grandfather's grave for the first time," he said, his voice husky with suppressed desire.

Removing the cap from the bottle, she poured them another drink. "Now this sounds like a story that'll take more than three questions to pry out of you. How about telling it in your own way?"

He took a deep breath, shifted on the cushions to ease his discomfort, and decided to humor her. "I flew up to Alaska to try to make amends to a beautiful lady because King Oil was responsible for hurting her birds. When I arrived, I discovered that my youngest brother, Dev, was already watching over Kristi like a hawk. At least he was trying to. Kristi had other ideas about how much protection she needed . . . but that's another story.

"Anyway, Dev nearly blew me out of the water when he told me the real reason he had flown to Alaska was to put a marker on our grandfather's grave. Here I had gone over to England to search for our roots, and I hadn't even bothered to find our grandfather's grave. Oh, we have a token marker in the family graveyard on the ranch, but my grandmother had insisted that his bones be buried in his beloved north. Leave it to Dev to find the grave, but I did help put up the marker. Well, I didn't actually get to put the marker on the grave, because an owl was nesting on it, and Kristi wouldn't let Dev go near it until the little owlet had flown. But—"

"—that's another story," Marnie finished with a laugh. "One I would dearly love to hear. So, how did you feel when you stood looking down at the grave?"

Strip poker would have been safer, less revealing, Duke thought, and wondered if he should pass off the question with a laugh. But it was an important question, one he hadn't faced honestly yet. "Empty inside," he said finally, raising unguarded eyes to meet Marnie's. "Because I knew that no grandson of mine would ever look down on my grave."

The pain in Duke's eyes called out to her, and Marnie leaned forward and brushed a kiss against his lips. A kiss full of sympathy, meant to heal his hurt. Instead, it lit a fuse inside her that fizzed straight to her heart. Startled, she sank back on her pillow and stared at him in confusion; he stared back, looking almost as confused.

And suddenly Marnie knew she would risk spending years of regret-filled, sleepless nights if she could somehow remove the pain from Duke's eyes, his heart, his soul.

"I know Karen hurt you badly," she said softly. "But isn't it time you were willing to believe in love again? To risk giving your heart once more?"

"I don't have a heart to give."

"I feel sorry for you, David King," she said, gazing at him with tears of tenderness in her eyes. "You might be the highly respected boss of a big empire; you might have the wealth and trappings to go with it; you might have the love of your family. But you are nothing unless you have a believing heart."

FOUR

"Teach my heart to believe," Duke whispered as he leaned forward and did what he had been aching to do all night—kiss her.

With a soft sigh she returned his kiss, and he pulled her down against him before she had second thoughts. When his lips commanded her to open her mouth, she obeyed, and his tongue quickly slipped inside.

Oh, Lord, how he needed her, Duke thought as he plundered her mouth. She tasted of scotch and honey, and he couldn't remember ever tasting such a heady combination. It shattered his self-control, and suddenly he needed to kiss her . . . until he didn't have the strength to kiss her again.

The need had been present the night before, he realized, partly masked by the drug, and it would still be there the next day if he didn't do something about easing it. So he kissed Marnie again, taking all the tenderness and compassion she was giving him and drawing it into the empty chambers of his heart.

His hands slipped under her sweater to caress the smooth skin of her back and brush the velvet of her breasts. She gave a soft, breathy moan and moved closer, making the sheet ride farther up his legs. Making him acutely aware of how little he was wearing. Making him achingly aware of how much he wanted her.

He shifted slightly, easing her body into a more comfortable position against his, and gave a fleeting prayer of thanks for the thick, plush pillows that were between him and the cold, hard floor.

A sultan couldn't have asked for a more comfortable bed . . . or a more willing woman to make love to.

Make love to!

With a muffled oath he raised his head and gazed into Marnie's gleaming eyes. Her cheeks were flushed, her lips swollen, and she looked so ready to love him that his breath caught in his throat.

He should be keelhauled for even thinking about making love to Marnie, he berated himself as he eased her off his body and onto the floor.

He continued to hold her arms, however, as he murmured, "Marnie, Marnie. This is madness."

Moistening trembling lips, she whispered, "Magical madness."

Giving in to temptation, he dropped another kiss

on her lips, then pulled back quickly. "All night long I've been telling myself that I shouldn't kiss you. And all the while you've been driving me to distraction with your beautiful smile, your happy laugh, and your bewitching wiggle. All night I've been answering your questions, and all the while I've been wondering what it would feel like if you wiggled when you're sitting on me—naked."

She drew in a shaky breath and wiggled again, then suddenly became aware of the cold floor beneath her. "Then why did you stop?" she asked, the words sounding more like a plea than a question.

Her eyes were glowing with desire, and for a moment Duke was tempted to say to hell with everything and take her. Take what he needed from her. And worry about facing himself in the mirror tomorrow—or when he finally got off this damn boat. But he couldn't do that.

"Because I don't want to hurt you," he said, raising his hand to trail his finger down her cheek. A frown marred her pretty forehead.

"How could your making love to me possibly hurt me?"

"Because I don't want to be like Jack and just use you," he said.

Marnie drew back and stared at him in dismay. "Zeus! I've done it again! A man says he needs me, and I lay myself at his feet."

"It wasn't like that at all," Duke objected with a

half-smile. "If anything, I was the one lying at your feet."

"You must think I'm a hussy."

"No way. You're a warm, wonderful woman."

"All I wanted to do was help you," she said, knowing even as she spoke that she had wanted more.

He raked a trembling hand through his hair, then gave her a stern look. "I don't need your help, Marnie. And I especially don't need your making love to me because you feel sorry for me."

"Make no mistake, Duke. I feel a lot of things for you, but pity isn't one of them," she said, then hid her burning cheeks against her upraised knees.

He reached out and touched her hair, but she sat silently, refusing to look at him. Finally, he eased his body off the pillows and walked, head bent, toward the companionway. He was pulling back the hatch when her voice stopped him.

"Where are you going?" she asked.

"To spend the night on the deck."

"Why in heaven's name would you do such a foolish thing?"

He shifted his stance, trying to disguise the fact that he still wanted her—badly. "Because there's only one bed on this boat, and after that kiss, I won't be responsible for my actions if I climb in it with you."

"I thought you didn't believe in love."

"You're right. I don't believe in love, but that

doesn't mean I won't turn down sex with a willing woman," he said in sudden exasperation, then gave her a slow, meaningful look. "Are you willing, Marnie?"

"Not to have sex," she said quickly.

"Then don't invite me into your bed."

She pushed herself to her feet and stepped into the forecabin, returning in a moment to dump a sleeping bag and blanket on the floor.

"Well, you don't have to go off on your high horse and sleep on deck. You can bunk down here on the pillows," she said, then stomped through the main cabin to the head. He barely had time to pick up the scotch and tumblers before she was making her way back to her bed. "And you don't have to worry about defending your honor. I'm not that starved for loving," she said, sliding the door shut with a decisive thud.

Duke stared at the door, feeling more battered than if he'd been worked over by his martial-arts instructor. Leaning down, he carefully straightened the pillows into a bed and arranged the sleeping bag on top. After giving the door another look of regret, he blew out the lamp and crawled inside the bag, propping his back up against the bulkhead—right next to the door he could open so easily. But he wasn't going to open it, he cautioned himself. Nor was he going to sleep. Not after what had happened—and had not happened—between them.

The tension was so thick on board the boat, it rivaled the fog outside.

"Marnie, I'm sorry, honey," he called softly. "I didn't mean to hurt you."

A deep sigh came from the other side of the thin wall. "It's all right, Duke. I warned you that I had a temper to match my hair." He heard the rustle of covers, and the boat swayed as she crawled to the bottom of the berth. Then she pushed the door open a crack. "Do you mind if we leave this open?"

"No. I prefer it that way," he said, and reached out to open it wider. Their hands touched, and he was surprised when she didn't pull hers away immediately. Her fingers brushed his knuckles tentatively, then withdrew, and he heard the covers rustle again.

"Duke, would you please sing to me?" she asked after she had finally settled down.

The tension had eased, but he still felt as if he should indulge Marnie a little. After all, she had indulged him a lot and had asked for nothing in return. Except that he bare his soul. "What would you like me to sing?"

"Anything. How about the song you sang when you were kidnapped."

"'The Wayward Wind?'"

She laughed softly. "That's the name of this boat, you know."

After a moment he began singing. Marnie listened to his rich, mellow voice, and felt like crying when she thought about the small boy who must have been so frightened all alone in the dark. The small boy who had been so courageous. The small boy who had grown up to be such a lonely man. As Duke sang the last notes, the foghorn echoed his refrain.

"I always thought the sound of an outward-bound train whistle was the loneliest sound on earth," Duke said slowly. "The foghorn beats it hands down. The outward bound calls to wanderers . . . and usually a man wanders by choice. The foghorn calls to lost souls . . . and a man has no control over what he loses."

Tears stung Marnie's eyes, and she pressed her fist against her lips to prevent herself from crying out. She caught a ragged breath, then another, and when she was sure her voice wouldn't break with emotion, she said, "Please sing some more."

He sang a cowboy ballad, then a love song, and finally "I Believe." And as she listened to the words, she wondered if she could help him believe again. For some reason Duke was hurting badly, and despite her vow not to become involved with a man who needed her, she was already committed to helping Duke—if he would let her. Because of the simple fact that she needed him.

For the first time in her life she knew what it was like to need a man. Never had she felt the excitement, the wonder, the breathless anticipation of making love. Nor the yearning ache of unfulfillment because she hadn't made love. And something in her heart warned her that she might never feel this way about a man again.

When he finally stopped singing, she lay silent, listening to the slap of the waves and the bellow of the foghorn, wanting so desperately to say something to him. To tell him how much his singing had meant to her. How much he had come to mean to her in such a short time. But she couldn't say any of those things. Not yet.

"Duke, are you asleep?" she whispered after what seemed like eons.

"Hmmm."

"What is your favorite color?"

"Sea green. And yours?"

"Silver gray."

Duke stood in the cockpit, staring at the island—or what he thought must be the island. The fog was so thick, he couldn't see anything recognizable, only a darker patch of gray.

"When is this fog going to lift?" he asked Marnie, who was at the bow checking the anchor. She came back toward him, her features taking shape as she drew closer. A yellow sou'wester was perched on her head, and she wore yellow deck boots. Her two pigtails bounced as she walked. How could Marnie look so warm and vibrant on such a dull, drab day? Duke wondered, then immediately answered his question. Because she was such a warm, vibrant person.

"Hopefully, it will clear tonight. I have to get home and feed the orphans," she said, smiling up at him. "Besides, I have to get you back to the resort. Your business associates will be worried sick about you. Do you think they've notified your family yet?"

"Lord, I hope not," Duke said, suddenly realizing how the news of his disappearance would affect his mother. "It took Madre years to get over my kidnapping, and I suspect she still lives in fear that it will happen again."

"They wouldn't necessarily think you've been kidnapped," Marnie said, trying to make him feel better.

"Yeah. Maybe they'll just think I drowned."

"Zeus! I never thought about that. I'm sorry, Duke."

Laughing huskily, he gathered her into his arms and gave her a hug. "Don't worry, Marnie. I'm sure things are under control. If Dare took the call, he'll move heaven and earth to prevent the folks from finding out what's happening. And if I know him, fog or no fog, he's already at the resort, keeping a lid on things."

Marnie nuzzled her face against his sweater, breathing in the exciting manly scent of him. "Thank you for being so understanding about this, Duke," she said, knowing she should be thanking him for a lot more. He could have taken her last night, but he had put his concern for her over his need for her. No matter what might happen between them before they got off this boat, she would never feel used. Duke was a good man, a man of integrity, a man she could trust.

Duke gazed into her sea-green eyes and wondered why he suddenly felt as if he wanted to stay there forever, with Marnie, shut off in a world of their own, with all the time in the world to make love.

But he wasn't going to think about making love with Marnie, he reminded himself sternly as he released her and stepped away.

"Would you mind if I took the dinghy and rowed ashore?" he asked, shoving his hands deep into the pockets of his black slacks. "I need to get off this boat for a while."

"Can I come along, or do you want to be alone?" she asked, hoping he didn't want the latter. She wanted to be with him as much as possible today.

He did want to be alone, and was surprised that he'd been so transparent. "Are you getting claustrophobic too?" he asked.

"I want to look for something to eat for tonight."

"Then by all means, come along. I wouldn't want to starve." He chuckled and added quickly, "Not that I'm complaining about the food. How you can manage to cook up gourmet meals on a two-burner stove is beyond me."

She smiled at him, pleased by the compliment,

but even more pleased to be going ashore with him. "If you'll bring the dinghy alongside, I'll collect the things we need and hang a light on the mast so we can find our way back."

Clarence was first to hop into the boat. They were soon loaded, and with Duke rowing and Marnie guiding them around the rocks, they reached the island without incident. The cat jumped out immediately and loped off down the beach, scaring a couple of squabbling gulls. Marnie climbed out and pulled the dinghy up on shore so Duke wouldn't get his boots wet again.

He stood on the tide-damp beach and peered into the thick mist, barely able to make out the towering fir trees and sprawling madronas that clung to the nearby cliffs. "Damn. I've heard of fog as thick as pea soup, but I've never been in it before."

"Fog is a magical, mystical fairyland West of the Sun and East of the Moon, where anything can happen and dreams can come true," Marnie said, swinging a pail that she had removed from the dinghy.

He shook his head, thinking that Marnie, with her wide eyes and pigtails, looked as if she belonged in a fairy tale. "Oh, Marnie, Marnie, you really are a dreamer!"

"I know, but I figure I have two choices. I can spend most of the winter feeling depressed, or I can make up stories and enjoy the rainy days and fog. I choose to enjoy."

"What I'd enjoy right now is a long run," he said, admitting to himself that what he would really enjoy was a long, slow session of making love with Marnie.

Something had made his eyes go soft and smoky, Marnie noticed, and turned away abruptly before she was tempted to find out what it was.

"There's not much hope of that, unless you want to run up and down the beach," she said, dumping her sou'wester into the dinghy. "But I'm afraid you won't get very far. There's not much beach here, even at low tide."

He took a step, felt the earth sway, and realized he wasn't in any shape to run anyway. It was going to take a while to get his land legs back.

Poor Duke, Marnie thought, watching him pace back and forth like a caged lion. He wasn't used to being cooped up on a thirty-two-foot sailboat. And now the fog was keeping him prisoner. It was a miracle he hadn't begun snarling at her.

She had visited this moorage at least once a month since she was ten, had explored the small cove and knew where the water was warmest to swim, the best stretch of beach for clams. She had climbed the tree-covered cliff that sheltered them from the strait and explored the rocks on the other side; had walked through the forest and played in the meadow. This was one spot where she had always been happy, and she wished that Duke could enjoy it too.

"You could use up some of your excess energy helping me dig clams," she suggested as she started off down the cobblestone beach toward the clam bed.

He caught up with her in two long strides. "And how much energy will that take?"

Not nearly enough, she acknowledged a few minutes later as she watched him wield the shovel. He dug as if possessed.

"Can't you dig any faster?" she teased as she tossed one clam that didn't get away into the bucket.

A burrowing clam spouted water in his face, and he paused to wipe it dry with the sleeve of his black sweater. "I thought clams were slow!"

"If you think these are fast, you should try digging razor clams on the West Coast. They disappear faster than roaches in a two-bit hotel when you turn on the lights."

"I would like to do that someday," he said, chuckling at the picture she painted. But only with her, he added silently. Because Marnie made even the most mundane experience seem like a great adventure. She was looking at him with a gamine grin on her face, and he laughed again. His laughter died as a feeling of gut-gripping need swept through him. Lord, how he wanted to reach out and touch her.

He was looking at her with hooded eyes, but Marnie could feel his need, feel how much he wanted to touch her. She stood her ground, resisting the compelling urge to throw herself into his arms, and was thankful—and disappointed—when he went back to work.

"Well, I think that's enough clams," she said when the pail was half-full. "Let's see if Neptune left a few more morsels lying around on the rocks."

After stashing the pail and shovel in the dinghy, Marnie picked up two plastic buckets, then held out her hand. "Will you hold my hand, please? We have to climb up over that cliff. I know my way up there blindfolded, but I don't want to lose you in the fog."

"What cliff?" Duke asked. Her hand was wet and cold, and he engulfed it in his, trying to warm it up.

"The one right in front of us." She waved at the long finger of land that had sheltered them from the stormy strait. "It's called MacBride's Mountain, and it's full of nymphs and druids. If we walk softly, we might be able to see them because they always come out to frolic in the fog. But beware, they'll play tricks on you."

"Aren't there any fairies?" he asked, intrigued.

"Oh, there are fairies, all right. You'll see them later when we go to Marnie's Meadow."

If anyone had told Duke a week ago that he had a vivid imagination, he would have pooh-poohed the idea. But when he and Marnie stepped from the beach into the trees, the fog swirled down around them, enclosing them in a mysterious wonderland. Waist-high sword fern seemed to bow down before Marnie as she followed an unseen path. Trees seemed to take the shapes of animals and birds and unknown spirits. As they climbed the hill, Duke was sure a devilish druid jumped on an evergreen limb and sent a shower of water down the back of his neck. And he became so engrossed in trying to catch sight of a shy nymph he thought was hiding behind a moss-covered log that he tripped over a half-buried root.

"See what I mean?" Marnie said, laughing at the sheepish expression on his face.

He laughed, too, and reminded himself that he didn't believe in fairy tales. But then, that didn't matter, because Marnie was magic enough for him.

All too soon they reached the rocky shore that was exposed to the waters of the strait. The foghorn boomed, and the sound surrounded them, providing an eerie kind of lament as they climbed out on the rocks.

"What are we doing here, anyway?" Duke asked, looking down at the icy blue-black water that swirled too near his feet for comfort.

Marnie pointed at the wedge-shaped shells that clung in clusters to the rocks. "We're gathering mussels."

Squatting down, he tried to pry one loose. "They're stubborn little so-and-sos, aren't they?" he said, then laughed as she blithely pulled off a handful and plopped them into the bucket.

"It's all in the way you hold your mouth."

The way she was holding her mouth made him want to kiss her, and he forgot all about gathering mussels. Instead, he stood and watched as she pursed her lips while she pulled on a shell, then smiled triumphantly when it came loose. Her lips were shining with mist of the fog, and her cheeks were rosy from the crisp autumn air; the space around her seemed to vibrate with energy. He leaned closer, drawn by the warmth.

"There, that should be enough," she said, glancing up at him. He loomed over her like a black creature that had just emerged from the sea, and for a fleeting second, Marnie felt as if he had come to take her to the Underworld.

She jerked in surprise, and her feet shot out from under her. With one quick movement Duke caught her and pulled her up against his chest. She felt his hand in her hair, heard the pounding of his heart, heard the answering thumping of her own heart.

"Dammit, Marnie, I just about lost you," he murmured into her hair, then took a deep breath. She smelled of the sea, and he knew that he would never smell that scent again without being reminded of Marnie. Slowly, reluctantly, he drew back slightly to look down at her.

"You frightened me," she said, smiling up at him.

"I'm sorry, Marnie. That wasn't my intention. Believe me."

It had been his intention to kiss her, Marnie realized, and the desire still ran rampant in his eyes—just as the desire raged in her veins. "It's okay, Duke, you couldn't help it," she said huskily, wishing he had kissed her, because that was what she'd wanted too. "There are forces all around us that are making things happen. Forces that we can't control."

"I'm always in control," he objected halfheartedly.

She held out her hand. "Let's go to Marnie's Meadow."

He took her hand and smiled down at her, totally unwilling to dredge up a logical reason for what was happening between them. "To look for fairies?" he asked.

"Mm-hmm," she said, her green eyes sparkling with happiness because he was entering into her fairy tale. "And on the way we'll stop off in Davie's Dreamland to see if there are any mushrooms. It's a little late in the year for them, but the weather has been unusual this fall, so keep your fingers crossed. Maybe we'll be lucky."

Davie's Dreamland, he discovered a few minutes later, was an old-growth forest, with Douglas firs towering so high above them that their trunks disappeared into the swirls of gray mist. But at their feet were the prettiest mushrooms he'd ever seen, golden-fluted trumpets that seemed to whisper something in his ear when he knelt down to examine them.

He listened, then glanced sideways at Marnie to see if she had heard them. She was carefully picking them, seemingly undisturbed, so it must have been his imagination, he told himself.

"Are they magic mushrooms?" he asked.

She gave him a bewitching smile. "Don't worry, they won't give you hallucinations or make you hear voices when you eat them."

"I wouldn't count on it," he said in bemusement. They were already talking to him, telling him to kiss her.

And when he and Marnie rose to their feet, he heeded the mushrooms' command. Wrapping his arms around her, he pulled her up against his chest, slanted his head, and kissed her. He savored her lips again and again until his senses were reeling, his heart pounding, and his blood singing with Marnie's music.

He lifted her off her feet, and she clung to him, returning his kisses as he dipped and turned in a slow circle. The fog swirled around them, shutting them off from everything else.

Feeling the last tattered remnants of his control give way, Duke slowly, reluctantly, lowered Marnie to the ground.

She sank against him and became totally aware of his arousal . . . and of the responding warmth and softness and ripeness deep inside her.

"Duke!" She drew back, laughing breathlessly. "What's gotten into you?"

Dazed, he shook his head and managed an equally breathless, "It must be mushroom magic."

"Or something else," she said, knowing the same thing was happening to her. Slowly, she held out her hand. "Come on, let's go to Marnie's Meadow."

"And what are we going to get there?" he asked as he took her hand and they began walking through the forest—Marnie carrying the mussels, Duke the mushrooms.

"Apples from the Garden of Eden."

"Apples out here?"

"Well, if you really want to know, this used to be an old farm before it was turned into a park. But I have always thought of it as my Garden of Eden."

Eden was a misty paradise, full of shadowy old trees, their gnarled limbs hanging with moss and memories of days gone by. They were happy memories, Duke sensed, of picnics, and laughing children, and starry-eyed lovers who had sat under them during the warm summer evenings, sharing dreams.

He followed Marnie as she drifted through the trees, drawn by the golden apples that glowed in the fog. Standing on tiptoe, she picked one, then took a bite.

"Delicious," she said, laughing as she wiped the juice off her chin. She raised the apple to his lips. "Here. Try it."

As his teeth sank into the apple, their gazes met and held, and each became totally, breathlessly, achingly, aware of the other.

This couldn't be happening, Marnie thought in

wonderment. She couldn't be falling in love with Duke. She had walked in her Garden of Eden many times before with a man, but he had been only a vague shadowy figure in her dreams. Duke was a flesh-and-blood man, with a face of a nobleman, the body of a buccaneer, and eyes that were looking at her as if she weren't quite real. Was Duke feeling it too? she wondered. And if by some miracle he was feeling the same way, would he admit it?

This shouldn't be happening to him, Duke thought in disbelief as he slowly began chewing the apple. He shouldn't be falling under the spell of Marnie's magic. He shouldn't be thinking of love and marriage and children—especially not children.

The longing in his eyes reached out to Marnie, but it was the battle raging in them that tore at her soul. She could almost hear one general shout, "Believe in miracles," while the other grumbled, "There's no such thing as love."

She also heard a little voice inside her urge, "Go on, Marnie, you can do it. You can take away his pain. You can make Duke's heart believe."

And this time she knew the reason she wanted to make Duke's heart believe was because she loved him.

FIVE

It was crazy to fall in love with Duke; he was only passing through her life, Marnie told herself, for the umpteenth time, later that evening as she gazed at him. He was wearing the white sheet again because his clothes had gotten wet during their walk. And once again he was lounging against the pillows, looking so regal despite his bare legs and feet, so sexy despite his skirt, and so very much like a god that she could scarcely believe he was real.

But he was real, and she loved him, and everything she'd learned about him in these two short days had made her love him more. And because she loved him, Marnie had also entered into the Roman-emperor fantasy, and had wrapped another sheet around her body and had piled her hair into a crown, allowing a coil to curl over her shoulder. When she'd emerged from the forecabin earlier, Duke had stared at her with raw hunger in his eyes, and the hunger was still there every time he looked at her during dinner. It disturbed her, making her wonder if she should go change. But something in his eyes also attracted her, making her feel weak with longing, making her feel tense with pent-up emotion, making her want to slowly remove his robe and spend the rest of the night exploring his long, beautiful body.

She had ached to start the exploration that afternoon while sitting up on deck, knowing that if she sneaked below, she'd catch Duke bathing. The memory of the hard, muscular body she'd seen when she'd stripped him the first night had created a tight knot in her stomach that wouldn't go away. And the knot grew tighter every time he looked at her.

The cabin was so full of sexual tension, it was a miracle it hadn't exploded, Duke mused, and knew that Marnie felt it too. She moved slowly, carefully, as if she were afraid the sexy sheet she wore would come apart at the seams. He loved the way it hugged the curves of her full breasts, her tiny waist, and rounded hips. But he also ached to unwrap the sheet and discover those very same curves for himself.

Lifting a forkful of mushrooms to his mouth, Duke chewed them slowly, then cocked his head and frowned in disbelief.

"Is something wrong?" Marnie asked.

Swallowing hard, he raised his gaze to Marnie's face and felt an almost overwhelming feeling of helplessness, as if some force were taking possession of his body, making him want to take Marnie in his arms and kiss her, to make love to her.

"Are you sure these aren't magic mushrooms?" he asked, looking at her with a mixture of disbelief and longing in his eyes.

"Only if you want them to be," she said, wishing that Duke would magically fall in love with her. Wishing that Cupid would shoot him with one of his arrows or that Venus would weave a spell over him.

He didn't want the mushrooms to be magic, did he? Duke mused. He didn't believe in magic mushrooms or spirits or gods. Did he?

Suddenly, Clarence stood up, arched his back, purred loudly, then bounded off to bed. But the spirits stayed, filling the boat with their presence. And with each mouthful of mushrooms Duke ate, the urge to kiss Marnie, to make love to her, grew stronger and stronger. And every time Marnie looked at Duke, the longing to make love with him became greater and greater . . . until her whole body was aching with need.

When Marnie got up and cleared away the remnants of their meal, Duke lounged back against the cushion-padded bulkhead and watched her. Silently, she gazed back, her emerald eyes glowing exotically, a mysterious smile on her lips.

"What's happening here?" he asked, the words a low rumble in his throat.

"You feel it too?"

"I feel something, all right."

"I'm afraid mere mortals don't stand a chance when the gods let loose their powers," she said, kneeling on the cushions beside him.

"I don't believe in gods," he said, leaning forward to take her in his arms.

Willingly, she nestled against his long, hard body. "No?"

"But if I did, I wouldn't have to look very far to find one, because you are Venus." Slanting his head, he kissed her with all the passion he'd been holding in check all evening, with all the burning desire that had coursed through his veins every time he'd looked at her.

And she kissed him back, ardently, feverishly, each kiss telling him how much she longed for him, needed him. How much she wanted to make love with him.

He felt her need, and it delighted him. Lifting his head, he gazed at her in concern. "I can't offer you anything, Marnie," he warned regretfully. "Words of love. Marriage. Any of the things a woman wants to hear."

"It doesn't matter, Duke. All I want is to make love with you."

"Then kiss me again," he commanded as he pulled her down on top of him, then rolled over so he was covering her body with his.

He covered her mouth with his, too, then groaned when she kissed him back. Her kisses were powerful, and her breathy little gasps were the most arousing sounds he'd ever heard. With another groan he tore his lips from hers.

"Lord, you're dynamite," he said with a growl, then smothered her murmur of protest with another hard kiss. "And if I keep kissing you, little Venus, it will be all over before we even begin."

She was ready for him, Marnie realized. His first kiss had turned her body into an open vessel. The second kiss had made her warm, and moist, and ready to receive him.

"Oh, Duke, Duke, I need you."

"So soon?"

"Oh, yes. I ache for you."

He gazed down at her, a pleased smile on his face. "Then we'll both have to ache for a little while longer," he said as he nipped a path of kisses across her cheekbone, then down along her jaw. "Because I want to taste all of you. You smell of peaches and taste like cream, and I want to eat all of you."

When he reached the tender skin of her neck, Marnie arched her head, giving him better access. His lips became greedy, and she felt as if he were going to devour her as his mouth moved inch by sensuous inch down her throat and into the valley between her breasts.

"As much as I like this gown you're wearing, it has to go," he murmured. Slowly, he loosened the knot at her side, eased down the white sheet, and gazed in admiration at her breasts. The lamplight bathed her skin in a golden glow, making him think of all the statues of goddesses he had seen, and knowing that none could compare to the reality of Marnie. "You, little Venus, are so lovely, you take my breath away."

Lowering his head, he took her nipple into his mouth, suckling it while his hand plumped and massaged her other breast. Each pull of his lips whispered through her, carrying golden droplets of desire. The droplets collected into a shimmering pool in the core of her being, and as he began kissing her other breast, the pool grew larger and larger until she was awash with desire. She rocked against Duke, wanting to feel his hard, muscular body against her, wanting to feel his surging power within her, wanting him . . . needing him.

Giving a soft little cry, she raised her head, searched for and found the pin that held his robe together. Releasing it, she gave a tug that left him gloriously naked. He was still arched over her, worshiping her breast. The muscles of his back and thighs rippled with restrained power, making her appreciate just how very masculine he was.

But when his manhood rested against her thigh, heavy, hard, and pulsing, his masculinity became heart-stoppingly evident.

"Oh dear, oh dear, oh dear," she said with such breathless wonder that he smiled down at her.

"Are you sure you still want to go on?"

"Oh, yes, yes, yes," she chanted.

"Thank God, because I don't think I could stop now."

She reached for him, caressing him, pulling him toward her. "I don't want you to stop," she said, her voice throbbing in her throat.

And suddenly he couldn't wait any longer. He had to be inside her, had to sink into her depths, had to feel her surround him completely. Despite his need, he entered her slowly and was glad he had, because she was so tight, he almost lost it then and there. She gasped, and he paused, waiting until her body accepted him.

"Marnie, are you all right? Did I hurt you?"

"I'm fine," she said on a wispy breath of air. "It's been a long time."

"For me too."

But as he stroked deeper into her velvety warmth, he realized he'd never felt this way before. Never felt so accepted, so welcomed, so very much at home. When he pushed higher, she willingly took him, asking for more. When he set up a steady rhythm, she wrapped her legs around him and arched her body against him until all he could feel was Marnie, both inside and out. She was Venus, he thought in wonder, the goddess of love.

He was her captain, Marnie thought, and she would sail with him to the ends of the earth. Because never before had she felt safe enough to let herself go, to give herself completely to a man, to let her lover take her through the stormy seas of passion into the sheltered waters beyond.

But never before had she been loved by Duke, and she continued to gaze at him with love in her eyes as she gave herself to him again and again. Then, still shuddering, still pulsing, she watched in fascination as he threw back his head, cried out, and gave himself to her.

Slowly, carefully, so as not to withdraw from Marnie, Duke eased onto his side and gathered her close. She snuggled against his chest, her breasts soft, her nipples firm, and he felt himself grow hard again from wanting her.

"Oh, Marnie, Marnie," he whispered huskily. "What's happened to us?"

"We made wonderful, glorious, marvelous love."

"We did, didn't we? I've never felt so happy in a woman's arms. So satisfied. So complete." He laughed softly in amazement. "And I've never lost control like that before, either."

She laughed softly in supreme contentment. "I warned you that mere mortals don't stand a chance when the gods let loose their powers."

He stroked her tiny waist and rounded hip, marveling at the satin smoothness of her skin. "I don't know whether it was the gods or the mushrooms . . . or you, little Venus, but I feel as if I'm in the Twilight Zone. And I'm afraid that when I wake up, I'll discover this was only a dream."

She trailed her fingers across his shoulders and back, tinglingly aware of his powerful muscles. "You call it the Twilight Zone. I call it the Land West of the Sun and East of the Moon. But whatever we call it, it is our world, where we can be one."

"We still are one."

Marnie felt him throbbing inside her and gasped as her body quivered in response. "In body, yes."

"And mind and spirit."

He spoke the truth, Marnie knew. Never before had she been so completely in tune with a man, as if she were thinking his thoughts, feeling his feelings, so totally surrounded by him that she didn't know where he stopped and she began.

"Yes, we are completely one," she whispered, and moved against him. "Isn't that wonderful?"

He splayed his hand across her bottom, pulling her even closer. "You're a sorceress, Marnie. You've cast a spell on me and made me forget about everything except making love to you."

"What else should you be thinking of?"

"That I should be protecting you," he said softly, then realized she would probably think he was worried about getting her pregnant, when he had really meant that he was worried about hurting her when he left. He should explain, he knew, but doing so would mean exposing his soul to her, and he couldn't do that, even after the lovemaking they'd shared.

"Oh, I'm safe. I'm taking the pill," she murmured, so drugged by him that she completely ignored the little voice in the back of her mind that was warning her that something wasn't quite right. She nuzzled her lips against his chest, tasting his salty skin. "Not that I've had much use for them until now."

He lay absolutely still, feeling as if his heart would burst. Marnie was such a mixture of innocence and seductiveness. Innocence that he'd felt the moment he'd entered her and that had made it pretty evident she hadn't been sleeping with Gil. Seductiveness because never once since his divorce had he been so bewitched by a woman that he'd forgotten to wear a condom.

"I just don't want you to be hurt," he said huskily.

She lay absolutely still as the knowledge that she was going to be hurt sank home. But she had known how he felt, she told herself, and the last thing she wanted to do was spoil the moment. "You can't hurt me, Duke," Marnie said bravely. "Because I don't want anything from you. Not words you don't want to say, or promises you don't want to keep. I only want to love you. Here. Now."

With a groan he rose above her again and proceeded to tell her, without saying one word, how he really felt about her. With a moan she urged him on, taking from him what he could give and giving it back to him a hundred times over.

And sometime during their loving, almost hidden by the bellow of the foghorn, came the tinkle of a fairy ringing her bell.

Marnie woke much later to the discovery that Duke was inside her once more, moving with the gentle rhythm of the rocking boat. Sleepily, she wrapped her arms and legs around him and pulled him deeper, and gave a ragged sigh when he filled her completely.

"I'm sorry, little Venus," he whispered against her lips. "I can't seem to get enough of you."

He began to withdraw, and she let him go slightly, then rocked against him. "Nor I, you. I don't want you to go."

He drew a shuddering breath and thrust into her until he felt as if he had touched her soul. "I'm afraid a lifetime of loving you wouldn't be enough."

She heard the desperation in his voice, and the need, and rocked under him again. She had no idea what was causing his pain, nor if she could help. All she knew was that, for some reason, he needed her.

Loving a man who needed her was dangerous, Marnie realized, but she also realized she had no choice in the matter. In this make-believe world David was her man and she was his woman. The real world could wait.

"Come to me, David," she murmured. "Let me give you a lifetime of loving."

With a cry of eagerness he plunged into her, and

she held him, wishing the moment would last a lifetime.

Duke stood on the deck and stared in awe at the sunlit scene before him. The inlet was a long bent arm of water, the deep blue middle rippled with silver, the edges dappled with a multitude of greens reflecting the tree-covered cliffs that sheltered it. "I never knew there were so many shades of blue or green," he said softly, gazing down at the woman who stood beside him. "And I've never seen anything so beautiful—except for you."

Surprised by his words, Marnie could only stand and stare at him. How could she have ever thought Duke King was cold?

"That's the nicest compliment anyone has ever paid me," she said, standing on tiptoe to brush a kiss against his lips. "Thank you."

Wrapping her arms around his waist, she gave him a hug, then lay her cheek against his chest, not wanting to move her body or the boat. Wanting, instead, to bottle their time together and save it to cherish when their passage was over, and her heart was shipwrecked in a sea of tears.

"I wish it were still foggy," she said wistfully, then straightened up and managed to give him a smile. "But the sun is shining and the wind is blowing, and I guess we'd better get under way."

She stepped back, gazed at him for another moment, then turned and walked toward the bow of the boat. He watched her go, feeling a crushing sense of loss. He realized how much Marnie had come to mean to him in such a short time and how hard it was going to be to walk away from her today.

"I'll give you a hand," he said, resenting the sunshine and steady wind. And when the sails were all up and trimmed, he leaned against the mast and stared pensively at the sea.

As they cleared the mouth of the inlet, Marnie called out to him, "I'll take you back to the resort."

"No. Head for home, Marnie. I know you're worried about the orphans. Besides, I don't want my adventure to end just yet."

"Then you can handle the tiller, and I'll sit back and relax," she said, sensing his sadness and wanting to do something to dispel it. She was not going to let the knowledge that Duke was leaving spoil this beautiful day.

Moving to the back of the cockpit, he took over the tiller and felt an immediate sense of renewed joy. The water was so blue, the tree-covered islands so lush, and behind him, on the mainland, a majestic snow-covered mountain reigned supreme against an azure sky.

"Is that Mount Baker?" he asked.

"The Indians call it the Great White Watcher. I find it comforting to know that it is always there, watching over me, even when it's raining or foggy and I can't see it."

"Oh, Marnie, Marnie. What else do you believe in?"

"I believe in you," she said, smiling at him.

He felt his heart leap and his loins stir, and he wondered if he would ever get over wanting her. "Damn. You're not supposed to say things like that."

"Because it embarrasses you?" Cocking her head, she studied him with wide, admiring eyes. He looked so handsome, despite his windblown hair and black beard, and so totally in control. "It's true, you know. You have an air about you that inspires confidence."

"Well, I sure as hell don't know how to sail this boat, and you'd better tell me what to do or we'll run into those rocks up ahead."

She laughed and told him, and a few minutes later remarked, "See? You handled that like a pro. We'll make a sailor out of you in no time."

"Why do you want to make a sailor out of me?"

"I have no ulterior motives, I assure you, except that I was hoping you might learn to enjoy sailing." They had so little in common, Marnie thought sadly, and she was a fool to think that things could be otherwise, but then, she had always been a dreamer.

"Well, I think you might be converting me," he said, knowing that what he was really enjoying was the opportunity of being near Marnie. This wonderful woman with her make-believe stories and her heartwarming belief in him had touched something deep inside, something that almost made him believe in himself.

He smiled at her, and when it became too painful to look at her any longer, he shifted his gaze to watch two black cormorants fly in formation, their long wing tips flirting with the waves. Overhead a bald eagle circled, and the sight of it almost took his breath away. But the feeling of heart-stopping breathlessness only happened when he looked at Marnie, Duke discovered, as he gazed at her again. And he wondered how long it would be before he could forget her. If ever.

Clearing the tip of the island, they tacked to run south. Duke spotted a tall ship coming toward them, her square sails full of wind.

"She looks like something out of *Mutiny on the Bounty*," he said, surprised to find himself longing for the good old days when sailing ships ruled the waves and a pirate could make off with the woman he loved.

"Isn't she beautiful? She's a brigantine, the *Silver Cloud*," Marnie told him. "Her owner lives in Seattle, but he brings her up to our boatyards for her annual maintenance. I fell in love with her the first time I saw her when I was twelve, and once I even stole aboard. Dad was a little upset when he had to go down to Seattle to pick me up, but I sure had fun pretending I could sail her anywhere I pleased."

Duke draped a hand across her shoulders and

smiled down into her eyes. "You mean you didn't pretend you were the beautiful princess who was on her way to the New World and was carried away by pirates?"

"Heaven's sakes, no. I was always her captain."

He laughed and hugged Marnie, then raised his hand to wave at the *Silver Cloud* as she breezed by. Marnie waved, too, and standing shoulder-to-shoulder, they half turned to watch the ship sail away from them.

"I would love to have the *Silver Cloud* for my sail-training program," Marnie said. "Learning to sail her would give the kids a real sense of adventure. Mind you, learning to work together is important, but my real goal is to help the kids learn how to dream."

He shook his head in amazement. "Marnie! Marnie!"

"I know, I know. I'm a dreamer. Even if Mr. Simpson would sell her, I couldn't afford to buy her. But if I did own her, I could take twenty-six trainees on board at one time. That's over twice the number I can take on the *Homeward Bound*."

"Don't stop dreaming, please," he said, bending his head to press a brief but adoring kiss on her lips.

She leaned against him, and they sailed in silence, glancing backward now and then until the *Silver Cloud* rounded the end of the island and sailed out of sight.

"There are a lot of kids in Houston who could benefit from such an experience," he said finally. "I coach an inner-city ball team."

Moving back slightly, she stared up at him in surprise. "You do? When do you find the time?"

"It's about the only think I do find time for, and I'm afraid I don't always make the practices or the games. A couple of other businessmen are involved in the project, so, among us all, we manage. But there's a hell of a lot more I could do, if I had the time and energy."

Marnie gazed at Duke, thinking that he was a very special man. How much more would he be doing, she wondered, if he had the support of a loving wife?

But she would never be his wife, she told herself, and was still telling herself the same thing as they made the final tack and headed for the MacBride Boatyards.

A half hour later Marnie led the way into the kitchen of her parents' white stucco house and pointed at the phone hanging on the wall.

"Why don't you make your call while I put on a pot of coffee, then I'll make mine," she told Duke, and gave him the number of the resort.

As Duke put through the call, he watched Marnie flit around the kitchen, measuring coffee and water into the coffeemaker, loading up a plate of spice cookies from a tin. She handed him one in passing, and he had just finished licking the tasty crumbs off his fingertips when the manager came on the phone.

After greeting Duke with relief, the other man asked him to wait for a moment, then a familiar voice rumbled along the line.

"Well, Big Brother, what the hell happened to you?"

"Dare! I thought you might show up," Duke said heartily.

"It isn't every day I get a chance to rescue you. In fact, I've never had that pleasure before. You've always rescued me."

"And you didn't need to come to my rescue this time."

"Like hell I didn't! I've been fighting fires since I arrived. The resort has been rampant with rumors . . . everything from your being kidnapped—I'm afraid the story about your kidnapping when you were a kid added more fuel to that fire—to your running off with a woman. At least I was able to keep a lid on the media. But what the hell's going on?"

"I . . . er went for a moonlight sail and got stuck in the fog for two days."

The line sizzled with silence. "Are you sure you're all right?"

"Yeah, I'm fine."

"I could have sworn you said you goofed off. You never goof off."

"I thought it was about time I had a little adventure." Duke chuckled. "Why should you hog all the danger and excitement, Dare?"

"You laughed! Now, I know for sure something's wrong. You never laugh."

"Well, I've laughed a lot these past two days," Duke said, and realized, to his amazement, just how much he had.

"What's her name?" Dare shot back.

Duke chuckled again, thinking, not for the first time, that Dare had inherited more than his brown eyes from their mother; he had also inherited her intuition. "Marnie MacBride."

"Do I get a chance to meet her?"

Duke met Marnie's startled eyes and grinned. "Yeah. If you'll fly over here and pick me up."

"I'll be there quicker than a hound dog can shake his tail."

After relaying Marnie's instructions on how to find the boatyard, Duke hung up, then took the cup of coffee she handed him and drifted over to the big oak table. He sat in the sunlight, half dreaming and half listening to Marnie as she phoned first Desiree and then her parents.

Marnie replaced the receiver and stood gazing at Duke, who was dozing in the sun. He looked so exhausted, she thought. It would do him a world of good to stay a couple of days so he could unwind, relax, and catch up on some much-needed rest. But that wasn't the only reason she wanted him to stay, she admitted honestly. She selfishly hoped that if he did stay, he would fall in love with her.

He stretched, yawned, and rubbed a weary hand over his face, then looked up to find her watching him.

"Sorry about that. The sun is so warm, I must have dozed off for a few minutes."

Smiling in concern, she joined him at the table. "You're tired, Duke. I wish you didn't have to rush home."

"I wish I could stay too." He shook his head, trying to clear it. "It feels as if I've been in a dream-world, and I don't want to wake up."

Marnie laughed softly. "I now know how Cinderella must have felt when her coach turned into a pumpkin." Noticing the guilty expression that clouded his eyes, she hastened to reassure him. "But I have no regrets about what we did last night, and given a chance, I'd make love with you again."

He smiled then, the smile she loved to see, the smile that had as much warmth as the sun.

"I feel the same way, little Venus," he said, leaning forward to take her hand. "There is no fog to cloud my vision, or mushrooms to work their magic, but right now I want to make love with you more than anything else in the world."

"Oh, David, so do I," she whispered, her heart leaping with renewed hope.

He gave her hand an apologetic squeeze. "But I must leave. I told you last night I couldn't give you the things you wanted and, unfortunately, reality hasn't changed because we've made love. I still can't make your dreams come true."

She stared at him, feeling as if a riptide were carrying her dreams away and there was nothing she could do to stop it. She had made love to Duke knowing that he didn't love her, knowing that he would be leaving. It wasn't his fault that she had built a fantasy around him.

"You're right," she said, and managed a smile. "This is the real world."

The *whack-whack* of chopper blades sounded overhead. "And reality is about to descend on us now," he said, releasing her hand and pushing himself to his feet.

She rose, too, and quickly headed for the bathroom. "You go and meet Dare and invite him in for coffee," she said over her shoulder. "I'll be out in a minute. A woman has to put on a pretty face when she meets a new man, you know."

"Your face couldn't be more beautiful," he called after her, then feeling as if he had lost something very precious, he went out to meet Dare.

Marnie splashed cold water on her face and pressed her fingers against her eyelids, trying to hold back the tears. She had never shed tears of self-pity before, and she wasn't going to now, she told herself sternly. The fantasy was over, and Duke was leaving.

The night before she had blithely assured him that he couldn't hurt her, but even then she had known she was stretching the truth.

She would carry the pain of Duke's leaving in her heart for the rest of her life. However, she wouldn't have done things any differently. Because nothing—not even her most sensual daydream— could compare with the reality of Duke's lovemaking. It was a memory she would cherish always.

Resolutely, she dried her face, combed her hair, and went to say good-bye to her love.

SIX

Lord help him, Duke thought as he listened to Dare's hurried words. He couldn't leave Marnie. Not now. Not after this new development.

"Someone phoned you and demanded a ransom?" Duke asked, staring at his brother in dismay.

Dare propped his shoulder against the black, green, and gold flag painted on the tail section of the King Oil helicopter, and hooked his thumbs in the pockets of his faded jeans. "Yeah. Right after I talked to you."

"I hope you told him where to go," Duke said, although he knew that Dare would have. Despite his easygoing appearance, Dare had a way of getting things done fast, efficiently, and with a minimum of risk. Traits that were essential when a man put his life on the line fighting oil-well fires.

"I did," Dare confirmed, shifting his weight so

he could toe a hole in the sand. "In four different languages, then wished I'd held my tongue."

"Why?"

"Because the man said that someone was going to pay, and pay dearly."

Duke ran an agitated hand through his hair as the implications of Dare's words sank home with a sickening thud. "Marnie!"

"You don't think she had anything to do with it, do you?" Dare asked, studying Duke thoughtfully.

"Hell, no!"

Dare nodded his head in satisfaction. "It's great to see that you're beginning to trust a woman again, Duke. There's hope for you yet."

Duke paced back and forth in front of his brother, not wanting to look at him, because looking meant he'd have to face King Oil's flag. The flag he had so proudly designed for the company as a symbol of hope. The flag that now symbolized his failure.

"Hope is for people who believe in happy-ever-after endings," Duke said, jerking his thumb toward the house. "People like Marnie. She rescued me from those men, you know, and now she's in danger."

"The authorities are looking for them, but they've dropped out of sight. Apparently, they've been in trouble with the law before, and there's no telling what they'll do next."

Duke stopped pacing and slammed a fist into the palm of his hand. "Damn."

"What are you going to do?"

"If I was sure it was just me they were after, I'd get the hell out of here, but it sounds as if they might come after Marnie. I can't leave her here all by herself."

"Do you want me to hang around?"

"No."

"Send in the troops?"

"No way. I'll handle this myself."

"Now I see why," Dare said, as the screen door banged shut and Marnie walked across the lawn toward them. He moved forward to stand beside Duke and told him in an undertone that was intended to be heard, "She is one gorgeous woman."

Marnie stopped a few feet from them and gave Dare a thorough once-over from his brown hair down to the scuffy toes of his boots. "My oh my, oh my," she said, patting her hand against her chest in the region of her heart. "Isn't he gorgeous? Isn't he enough to make a woman's heart go pitter-patter? Isn't he a man to die for?"

Dare threw back his head and laughed, then laughed even louder when Duke, too, began laughing.

"Aren't you going to introduce me to this handsome hunk of a man?" Marnie asked, trying to keep a straight face.

"Marnie, meet my brother Darrick. Dare, this is Marnie MacBride."

She stuck out her hand, but Dare ignored it. Placing his large hands around her waist, he lifted her easily, covered her squeal of surprise with his lips, then lowered her to the ground.

"Marnie, it's a real pleasure to meet a woman who has such good taste in men," he said, grinning down at her. "Especially when she can also make my brother laugh."

Marnie fanned her burning cheeks, but she wasn't willing to admit defeat. "Tell me, Dare." She batted her long lashes at him. "Did your mother break the mold when she had you, or is her third son even taller and handsomer?"

Dare cocked his head, pretending to give his answer serious consideration. "Dev's handsomer, but it's a toss-up whether he or Duke is the runt of the family."

Marnie's eyes softened as she turned to look at Duke, who was watching them with a pleased smile on his lips. "Some runt," she said, unable to keep the admiration out of her voice. She continued to look at Duke for a long moment, then swallowed hard. "Do you have time for coffee, Duke, or do you have to leave?"

"I was just telling Dare I really didn't want to go," Duke said tentatively.

"And I was telling him he should hang loose for a few days," Dare said, smiling at Marnie. "You know, it's about time this big brother of mine took a vacation. He hasn't had one in years."

"Oh, Duke, could you stay?" Marnie asked, hardly daring to hope she might get a chance to win his love. If only she could have a few more days with him.

He wanted to stay, Duke admitted, not only because he wanted to protect Marnie, but also because he wanted to be with her. There was something in Marnie that drew him—an inner warmth, a generous, loving nature that made it almost impossible for him to leave. Which was the very reason he should. Or at least make a pretense of leaving, and then come back and watch over her from a distance.

"I don't know," he said, fighting a losing battle with his conscience. "I should really get back to work."

"I'll keep an eye on the Baron," Dare said quickly. "Besides, tomorrow is Thanksgiving, and Madre will make good and sure he doesn't go near the office."

"Oh, my gosh, Thanksgiving! I forgot all about Thanksgiving." Marnie stretched out an imploring hand to Duke. "Oh, Duke. Duke. Can you carve a turkey?"

Bewildered by Marnie's apparent distress, Duke reached out and took her hand. "Ah, yes."

"He's the best carver this side of the Pecos," Dare boasted.

"Then you have to stay," Marnie said, giving Duke's hand a little squeeze. "I need your help, desperately. A dozen special friends are coming for dinner tomorrow. It's a tradition, you see, and I assured Mom and Dad that I would carry on even though they're away. I can cook the meal—in fact, I always cook the meal because Mom doesn't cook—but I cannot carve the turkey."

"You make your living working with knives, but you can't carve a turkey?" Duke asked, shaking his head in surprise.

She gazed up at him earnestly. "I take one look at it and remember when it was strutting around the yard, and I can't bear to stick a knife in it. I tried one year, but I started to cry and wound up slicing my hand, and it bled so much, it ruined the dinner."

"Oh, Marnie, Marnie," Duke said, laughing softly.

"I know you'll think I'm a bubblehead, and I am a bubblehead, because I forgot all about the carving sooner, but—"

"Ssh," Duke said, placing a finger over her lips. "I don't think that at all."

"Then you'll stay?"

"Yes, I'll stay," Duke said, feeling the same sense of unreality that he'd felt in the fog. And the sun was shining. "Besides, I want to see if I can make your dream come true."

What dream? Marnie wondered as Duke slowly released her hand and stepped away from her. She stared at him, vaguely aware that Dare had taken his place.

"Good. Now that's settled, I'd better hit the

road," Dare said, smiling down at her. "But before I go, I want to tell you, Marnie, you're the best thing that's come down the Pike." Leaning over, he gave her a hug. "Thanks for turning my brother back into a human being. I'd almost given up hope for him." Turning his head slightly, he whispered into her ear, "Maybe you can make his dreams come true too."

"I'll try," she whispered back, then stood in a daze, watching as Dare unloaded Duke's suitcase, gave his brother a rib-cracking bear hug, then climbed into the helicopter and flew away.

Was Duke talking about her dream of having children? Of having a husband who loved her?

She turned to look at Duke, her eyes shining. "What dream?" she asked.

He stared into her eyes, wishing he could make all her dreams come true, then looked away quickly because he knew he couldn't.

"Your sail-training program," he said huskily. "But I'd like to learn more about that before I make a final decision about funding it."

Swallowing her disappointment, Marnie gave his arm a little hug. At least she would have some more time with him. And miracles did happen— once in a blue moon. "Come on then, let's go see *Homeward Bound*."

"I'm impressed," Duke said as he jumped off the deck of the *Homeward Bound* and landed on the dock.

Marnie landed nimbly beside him and lovingly ran her fingers along the side of the sleek fifty-foot schooner, which had been hauled out of the water. "We could launch her anytime," she said proudly. "We're just finishing the paint job."

"How much is she worth?"

"A couple of hundred grand if I were to put her on the market. But I'm not about to do that after all the hours of hard work I've put into her. Besides, I didn't restore her to sell her. She's going to be the flagship of the program. We can sail her with a crew of three and take up to a dozen trainees on board."

"How much will it take to operate the program?" Duke asked, smiling at her enthusiasm.

Marnie named a figure, then added, "Come into the office and I'll show you the proposal. I'm sorry I didn't bring it along with me to the resort. Another case of being a bubblehead, I'm afraid. I'm sure you're beginning to wonder if I'm safe to let loose with a bunch of kids. I might forget to bring them back."

Shaking his head in amusement, Duke followed her into the office, but a few minutes later he was shaking his head in admiration. "As I said before, you're not a bubblehead," Duke told Marnie. "This proposal is one of the best I've ever seen, and most of those have been written by professionals who make a living submitting proposals."

"Thank you," Marnie said, glowing under his unexpected praise.

"But you'd be better off selling *Homeward Bound* and recouping the money you spent on her."

"Money isn't all that important to me. Help—"

She smiled at him sheepishly, realizing she must sound like a bleeding-heart do-gooder.

"Helping people is," he finished for her, and gave her a smile that brought more color to her already rosy cheeks.

"Yes."

Placing the report on the desk, he took her hand and led her back outside, then stood looking thoughtfully at the sheds, the hoists, and the cradles that held two boats in various stages of construction. "Your father has a lot of money tied up in this business."

"He's been a shipwright for forty years and is known worldwide for his wooden yachts," Marnie said proudly.

Duke pointed at an old skiff with cracked ribs lying against one of the sheds, and a tugboat that was heeled over on the beach, its pilothouse askew. "And what about those old wrecks?"

"They're an eyesore, I know. Dad's embarrassed to have them cluttering up his beautiful boatyard. They give people the wrong impression."

"Why am I beginning to think they belong to you?"

"Because they do." She paused, looking slightly embarrassed. "You see, every time I come across an old derelict, I have to haul it home. They have so much history. The skiff, for example, was built in 1929 by a fisherman. His wife and children were drowned in a freak storm, and he took out his remorse on the boat. I figure that with a little TLC, I can fix her up again and change her luck."

Duke gazed at Marnie, wondering if she would ever cease to amaze him. "Did *Homeward Bound* and *Wayward Wind* look like these boats when you brought them home?"

"Well, not much better."

He lifted her hand, turned it over, and brushed a kiss against her palm. "I stand in awe, Marnie, of the miracles your TLC can work," he said huskily. "And I'll gladly give you the money for your program, without any conditions attached."

Marnie flung her arms around Duke's neck, pulled down his head, and kissed him. "Oh, thank you, Duke," she said, and kissed him again.

Belatedly deciding that she shouldn't be kissing a man for giving her money, Marnie released Duke and stepped away. She couldn't, however, stop herself from beaming at him.

He smiled back, looking a trifle disconcerted and a whole lot endearing, and it was all Marnie could do to remember that she shouldn't be kissing him.

"Giving money is the easiest part of any project," he said sincerely. "Making it work is much harder. However, I have no qualms that you'll make it work, Marnie."

"Still, if I didn't have your money, it would be

almost impossible to launch the program. I wish there was some way to thank you properly."

"You already have." Raising his hands, he cupped her face and gazed earnestly into her eyes. "And I'm not talking about the generous way you gave me your body either. There is not enough money in the world to pay you for that gift." His thumb caressed the corner of her mouth, coaxing it into a pout. "I'm talking about the way you've made me feel young again, made me feel like kicking up my heels for the first time in my life, made me feel like saying to hell with the world, I just want to be here with you. At least for as long as I can."

If she had her way, he would stay forever, Marnie thought. "Damn," she said softly.

"What's the matter?"

"I don't know why I was in such a hurry to show you the boat. There's no longer any reason for you to hang around."

"Are you saying that now you've got what you wanted, you're going to throw me out?" he asked, teasing her gently.

"Duke. Never. You can stay as long as you want."

"Thank goodness you said that. There are so many other things that I want to do before I leave."

"Such as?"

"Kiss you. See the orphans. Kiss you."

Lowering his head, he kissed her, marveling at

how kissing Marnie could make him feel so good. He couldn't seem to get enough of her.

"Marnie," he murmured against her lips.

She opened her luminous eyes and gazed at him. "Hmm."

"I think we'd better go feed the orphans."

The orphanage, Duke discovered a few minutes later, was a fenced enclosure that contained holding tanks in the water, a big, rambling barn, and wire cages of various sizes and shapes. Marnie led Duke to the holding tanks, where she introduced him to two harbor-seal pups who greedily accepted the fish she gave them.

"We had a half-dozen this summer, but Binkie and Boss are the only two left. Binkie, unfortunately, is blind, so I won't be returning her to the sea. An aquarium in Seattle has agreed to take her, and I'll send her as soon as Boss is ready to go home. He belongs over there on one of the Canadian islands." She waved a hand at the islands to the west of them. "The fishermen who found him brought him here because we were close. Poor Boss had been hit by a speedboat. It was a miracle he survived." Leaning over, she scratched the seal's head as he looked up at her with big, dark, watery eyes. "I try not to handle the animals too much, especially when I know they'll be going back to the sea, but in Boss's case, I couldn't help it." Binkie butted her head against Marnie's arm, demanding her share of petting. "And of course Binkie is a real sweetheart. Do you want to pet her?"

The real sweetheart was Marnie, Duke thought as he reached out and touched the seal's sleek head. She was so warm, so loving, so giving. No wonder the seals wanted her to pet them. Marnie handed him a fish, and he fed it to the seal, and from there it seemed natural to feed the seals a few more fish, talk a little nonsense to them, and pet them again before he followed Marnie to the barn.

They were met by a dainty fawn. "This is Delight," Marnie said, stroking the animal's velvet nose. "She's still on the bottle. For some reason she was born very late in the season, and then her mother died. I've had her since she was a day old, and I probably won't release her until next spring. Would you like to feed her while I look after the other animals?"

"Sure, I'll give it a go," Duke said, and sat down on a pile of straw. The fawn approached shyly, head down, nostrils quivering, but when Marnie handed Duke the bottle, Delight was quite content to suck the nipple. And when Duke reached out a hand to pet her, she sidled closer to his touch.

Marnie watched them for a moment, impressed by how gentle Duke was with the animal, and at how quickly Delight had accepted him. He was a high-powered businessman, but he had adapted very quickly to the slow pace of her island life. She knew he wouldn't be content to remain here forever, but right now he needed the break from his hectic schedule, needed the time to relax and enjoy the simple things in life. And if she could give him the respite he needed, then she would be content.

Slowly, she turned away and walked toward a wooden cage. "Rusty, here, had a run-in with a car," she said as she opened the door to reveal a roly-poly raccoon with bandages on his leg. "His cast is due off in ten days, but he'll be with us until he regains his strength. We had a hard time with him. He kept chewing off his cast, but we finally convinced him that he had to leave it alone."

"You used a little magic on him, did you?" Duke said softly, smiling at her.

"Yep, I waved my wand, and he behaved," Marnie said. They continued to smile at each other until Delight bunted the bottle, demanding Duke's attention. The smile he turned on the fawn made Marnie feel like toasted marshmallows inside, and her voice was husky with suppressed emotion when she spoke. "Looks as if someone else is working magic."

A pleased little grin tugged at the corner of his mouth. "She seems to like me," Duke whispered, sounding surprised.

"I wonder why?" Marnie said, fighting the urge to kneel down beside Duke and kiss him. When the urge was under control, she put fresh water and food into Rusty's cage, then moved from cage to cage, naming the animals and birds inside and telling Duke their stories. And all the while she kept sneaking looks at Duke's black head, which was bent close to the fawn.

When the bottle was empty, Duke gently removed it and let the fawn suck on one of his fingers. The fawn chewed for a while, then nibbled his sweater, and finally raised her head to nuzzle Duke's cheek. Laughing softly, Duke nuzzled back.

Marnie stopped what she was doing and stared at them, realizing how much she loved Duke. She loved him totally, unreservedly, unquestionably. She loved him regardless of the fact that he didn't really belong there, didn't want her in his life—and hadn't even told her that he loved her. Although she had known him only a few days, it seemed as if she had known him forever. And she had, Marnie realized, because Duke had been part of her life from the day she had first begun to spin her own fairy tales about kings and knights and pirates. Duke was her beloved pirate, her shining knight, her noble king. And she loved him with all her heart and mind and soul.

Gradually, she became aware that Duke was looking at her as if he was expecting an answer.

"I'm sorry," she said, and gave a short laugh of embarrassment, hoping he hadn't guessed what she had been thinking. Because if he knew, he'd be in his helicopter, flying back to Texas quicker than a flea could jump onto a dog.

Duke smiled at her. "I said I guess I'm finished here. Is there anything else I can do?"

You could love me, Marnie thought, and bit her lips to keep from blurting out the words. Turning away abruptly, she began searching through the bags of feed until she realized she didn't know what she was looking for. She took a deep breath, then turned to face Duke again. "We have to feed the birds outside, then we can go clean up."

The three gulls squabbled over the food Marnie threw them, and Duke was still laughing at their actions as they approached the final cage. It held a long-legged blue heron that did not look happy, even when Marnie dumped a pail of fish into the enclosure.

"Blue Boy was starved when we got him because he had a fishing line wrapped around his neck. He's only been here a week, and he's almost ready for release."

"You name a bird even though it's only going to be here a few days?" Duke asked in surprise.

"I give every bird or animal that comes into the refuge a name and make up a story about it."

"Which all have happy-ever-after endings."

"Of course."

Raising his hands, he placed them on her shoulders and gazed down at her, his eyes mirroring his concern. "Marnie, our story isn't going to have a happy-ever-after ending."

Unperturbed, she smiled at him. "So you say."

He shook his head. "Lord, I should be shot for

staying here with you. I should have left with Dare. I should have—"

"Sssh," she said, reaching up to brush a quick kiss across his lips. "I'm glad you stayed. You weren't ready to go back to your world yet."

Slowly, he released her and stepped back, forcing down the almost overwhelming urge to take her in his arms and never let her go. "This isn't a fairy tale, Marnie. I will be returning to my world. And I don't want you to be hurt when I go."

"I know you have to leave, David, and when you do, I'll let you go," she said, hoping her actions would be as brave as her words when the time came— if the time came. "Just as I let these orphans go when they're ready."

"And what kind of story will you make-believe about me?" he asked softly.

Marnie thought about all the dreams she wanted Duke to be a part of and then pushed the selfish thoughts aside. She reached out and placed a hand on his arm. "That you will fall in love with a woman who will make you truly happy and have lots of children."

For a moment he stared at her as if his world had come to an end, then his features grew hard, his eyes cold, and he wheeled away. She gazed at his back, wishing she knew what she'd said to hurt him.

"David. You will be happy," she said earnestly. "If only you will believe in yourself."

He took a deep breath, gave a half-laugh, and

turned to face her again, attempting a smile. It was ragged and bittersweet.

"You are an incurable optimist," he said huskily, and leaned over to brush a kiss against her lips. He raised his head and smiled at her, and this time his smile made the grade. "I'll take that shower now. I've been looking forward to it for days."

"Do you want to stay at the house or with me?" she asked, her eyes still full of concern.

"You don't live with your parents?"

"I moved out years ago." A tiny smile flirted at the corners of her mouth. "They needed their privacy, you see."

"Then by all means, I want to stay with you."

After they had stopped by the house to pick up Duke's suitcases, Marnie led him along a wooded path that followed the shoreline and then down a hill into a secluded cove.

Duke knew immediately where Marnie lived. A lone boatshed sat on the middle of a pier, but it was no ordinary boatshed. The upper portion of the whitewashed walls had been replaced by windows, and solar panels and skylights lined the steeply pitched green roof. A stained-glass window in the oak door welcomed them home, and as they stepped onto the pier, Duke saw the words SEA SHANTY had been carved above the curving glass.

"I should've known," he said, smiling at Marnie in delight.

Marnie smiled back. "When I told Dad I wanted

to move out, he offered to build me a cottage with all the mod cons, but this old boathouse had been sitting empty for so long, and I felt so sorry for it, I decided to fix it up. Dad swore it would've been cheaper to build a house from scratch."

"It's beautiful, Marnie. And you can't get any closer to the water without being on it." Glancing over the edge of the pier, he realized that only four feet of boards showed above the water. "Aren't you afraid you'll be flooded out?"

"No. It's a floating pier, so it goes up and down with the tide, and there's lots of space under it for the floats. The bay is sheltered so we don't get battered by storms, and the boards keep the logs and other debris out from under the house."

"Wouldn't it have been easier to live on a house-boat?" he asked, then held up his hand when she opened her mouth to answer. "I know, I know. You haven't found one that needs you. Right?"

She tried not to grin but failed. "Right."

"And what would you do with this shanty if you found a boat that needs you or a man who loves you?"

"I have any number of friends who are itching to either buy or rent it."

He glanced out at the mouth of the bay, where the sun would set, then back at the meadow, where the deer would graze at sunrise. An eagle soared overhead, sea gulls floated nearby on the water, and at the end of the pier a cormorant sat on a piling with its wings hung out to dry.

"I can see why. It's beautiful here, so peaceful. I wouldn't blame you if you stayed put for the rest of your life."

"A view isn't everything. I was willing to go to Houston, but Jack never asked me to go with him."

"I still say the man was crazy."

Embarrassed, she ducked her head. "I want you to know that you're the first man I've ever brought here."

"Not even Jack?" he asked in surprise, reaching out to take her hand.

"No. You see, we never had a flaming affair. It was more of a high school romance, and when he went away, I decided I didn't want to be one of the women he visited in his many ports of call. I wanted more, and I kept hoping he wanted more too."

He squeezed her hand. "Marnie," he said, not knowing what else to say.

She gave a slight shake of her head. "Anyway, I wanted you to know."

Turning, she opened the door and led the way into her home. Duke followed, feeling more humble than he'd ever felt in his life. Then he blinked in surprise as he looked around.

Except for the bathroom, which stood midway down the wall on the right, it was one big room. The kitchen lay between the door and the bathroom, the bed beyond, with the in-line dining room and living room taking up the rest of the space. It was more like a greenhouse than a home, with ferns hanging from the beams, ivy growing around the pillars, and potted palms screening off the bed. White wicker furniture and braided green rugs were scattered over the oak floor, and two Bentwood rockers were drawn cozily up in front of a gleaming black potbellied stove.

"It's beautiful, Marnie," Duke said, realizing she had been waiting for him to comment. "But don't you feel as though you're sitting in a showcase?"

She turned in a slow circle, arms spread, then hugged herself in delight. "Ah, but that's where I splurged. The windows are state of the art; they're treated so the house won't get too hot in the summer or cold in the winter and, best yet, so no one can see in, while I can see out."

He couldn't help but chuckle at her enthusiasm. "No wonder your friends all want you to get married!"

The thought that she might never get married sobered her, and turning away from Duke, she pointed toward the bedroom. "You can put your suitcases in there, and if you want privacy, all you have to do is drop the screens." Moving to the pillar nearest the kitchen, she pressed a button, and a gauzy curtain swished down from the beams, completely enclosing the bathroom and bed.

"State of the art," he said, echoing her previous words in admiration.

"There's just one thing," she said, suddenly remembering how claustrophobic Duke was. "The bathroom is a trifle small. Perhaps you should have showered at the house."

"I'll manage," he assured her hastily, because there was no way he was going to let her out of his sight if he could help it.

"Then, if you don't mind, I'll take mine first and make lunch while you're having yours."

She hurried her shower, not allowing herself to dwell on the fact that she had invited Duke to stay with her in her home. For the first time in her life she would take a lover into her bed, and she wondered how she would feel about living in her home after he was gone. But she wouldn't think about that now, she told herself as she toweled dry and began brushing her hair. She would think about loving Duke.

The happy thoughts lasted until she pulled open the door of the medicine cabinet and saw the disk of birth-control pills. With a sinking feeling, she realized that in her haste to leave for the resort, she had also forgotten to take her pills along. Picking up the disk, she discovered that she had missed four days. Her heart skipped a beat, and she turned over the package and read the precautions. It wasn't safe to start taking them again, she decided, because she might, even now, be pregnant, and she didn't want to do anything to harm the baby. She took a deep breath, then another, telling herself that she was probably worrying needlessly. And she certainly wasn't going to tell Duke, not after reassuring him that she was protected. He would think she was a real bubblehead. Besides, she didn't want to spoil the rest of their time together.

And if, by chance, their wonderful loving had made a baby, she would definitely tell Duke. He would understand, wouldn't he?

Duke sat on Marnie's king-sized waterbed—which was nestled like a pearl between two lustrous, scallop-shaped bedsteads—thinking about how much he was looking forward to making love with her, even though that wasn't the reason he'd stayed. However, he was beginning to suspect that she didn't need his protection either. Everyone on the islands must love her, and if he was honest with himself, he'd have to admit that he did too—a little.

And everything he learned about Marnie made him fall deeper under her spell. Obviously, the Mac-Brides were well off, yet Marnie chose to live simply in a one-room boatshed. Marnie didn't have to work, but she did. Marnie could go anywhere in the world, yet she chose to stay here and help mixed-up kids learn what was important in life.

And if she was able to instill half of the values she held dear, the kids would have a chance to make something of themselves.

Marnie, he realized, enjoyed life to the fullest, and when there was nothing to enjoy, she created a make-believe world where everyone's dreams came true. And selfish or not, for a few more days he would stay with her in her fantasy world and dream.

She emerged from the bathroom wearing a silk robe hand-painted in a seascape of greens and blues, a towel around her head, and a warm, loving smile. Duke rose to his feet, wanting to start the fantasy then and there. Instead, he gave her a half-smile, picked up his clean clothes, and walked into the bathroom. He shut the door, then opened it immediately. "Would you mind if I left this open?"

"Go ahead. And use all the hot water you want. It's solar-heated, and we have plenty."

The need to make love with Marnie was so great that he didn't intend to waste a second in the shower. He was standing with a towel knotted around his waist, splashing shaving cologne on his tender neck when he heard a thump and bang coming from beneath his feet.

Poking his head out of the bathroom, he called to Marnie, who was clanging pots in the kitchen. "Marnie. What's the noise in here?"

She came to him, laughing, a piece of cooked chicken in her hand. But the laughter died when she saw him. "My, don't you look good enough to eat," she whispered huskily.

His lips quirked into a pleased little smile. "It looks as if you've already got something to eat."

"Oh." She lowered her gaze to her hand. "No. This is for Selina. She's come begging for food.

Step out of the bathroom so I can open the door for her."

He stepped out, and as she moved past him, she couldn't resist the temptation to trail her fingers across his hair-covered chest.

He sucked in a startled gasp. "Behave yourself, Marnie," he warned.

She shot him a saucy grin. "I'm not doing anything."

"Except stroking a lion."

"And feeding an otter."

Bending over, she lifted a trapdoor that had been skillfully cut into the tiled floor. He moved to help her but realized that she didn't need any help; the door lifted easily and silently. An otter appeared in the opening and climbed up onto the tiles. She greeted Marnie with a chirp, then took the piece of chicken between her paws and began eating daintily.

"Selina lives under the house and keeps me safe from the underworld," Marnie explained, smiling up at him. "When she has her pups, she brings them up to visit. She'd move right in with me if I'd let her, but that would put Clarence's nose out of joint."

Duke stood silently, gazing down at Marnie while she fed the otter, then sent it away with a loving pat. Replacing the door, she stood up and washed her hands at the sink. She turned, a smile on her face, but it faded when she saw the expression on his.

"Duke. What's wrong?"

"Nothing is wrong, little Venus. Except that I suddenly find I'm very jealous of a one-eyed, three-legged cat and an otter."

She stepped toward him and wrapped her arms around him. "Oh, Duke. Duke. I have lots of love left over for you."

"Good. Because I want some of it right now," he said as he swept her into his arms and carried her toward the bed.

SEVEN

Duke woke and found that the sun was setting, and he was alone in Marnie's bed. He smiled in satisfaction as he remembered the erotic way the bed had moved while they were making love.

"Marnie, are you out there?" he called, raising his head to look around. A light glowed in the kitchen, but the shanty was empty. Marnie couldn't have gotten far, he decided, and gazed out the window, wishing she had stayed so they could enjoy the sunset together. The fresh, light scent of lavender still lingered on her pillow, and he clutched it to his chest as he watched the large golden ball sink into the sea. Never before had he seen so many shades of pink and mauve and red, he thought, but never before had he taken the time to see a sun actually set. Never before had he felt so relaxed and refreshed, because never before had he experienced Marnie's special brand of TLC.

She had said she had enough love for him, and then had proceeded to prove it in a way that, even now, had the power to stir him. She had given him so much, and although she had satisfied him completely, he realized he needed her again. And he was afraid he would go on needing her for a very long time.

But what about Marnie? he wondered. Lord, he hoped she hadn't really meant she was in love with him. Thoughtfully, he watched the color fade out of the sky. Sure she loved him, he reasoned, but she loved broken boats and injured animals, too—because they needed her. She had sensed his need and was responding to it, and although he had told her he didn't need her, he had lied.

He could only hope and pray she hadn't been lying, too, when she'd assured him that he couldn't hurt her. But hadn't she also told him that she never lied? he asked his nagging conscience. Besides, there was still a chance she might need him—at least his protection.

Neither argument helped to assuage his guilt, and flinging off the comforter, he rolled out of bed. Feeling a trifle exposed with all the windows—even though Marnie had assured him that no one could see in—he pulled on his slacks before wandering into the kitchen.

Marnie's note on the counter read, *Hi, sexy! Hope*

you've had a nice nap. You'll need your strength for
tonight. Meanwhile, if you want to join me, I'm at the
main house in the kitchen. Oh, yes, would you please feed
Selina if she comes calling.

His good humor restored, he headed for the
bathroom. If Marnie had loving on her mind, he'd
need a long, hot shower, and maybe another shave.
Unwilling to waste any of his precious time with her,
he cut the shower short and was combing his hair
when a thumping came on the trapdoor. Kneeling,
he opened it. When Selina came up, he fed her and
petted her and found himself talking to her.

"So you're the guardian of the underworld, are
you? It sure is a black hole," Duke said, staring
down at the oily water. There was a good two feet of
headspace between the surface and the pier, he
noted. Lots of breathing room for an otter or a man
who didn't have claustrophobia. "I don't blame you
for wanting to stay up here with Marnie and soak up
her love," he continued as he gave the otter one final
pat, pushed her toward the hole, and closed the
door. "Because that's what I'm going to do right
now."

Dressing quickly in black slacks, sweater, and
jacket, he walked through the trees toward the beck-
oning light in the kitchen window of the main house.

"Come on in," Marnie called out in response to
his knock, and turned to greet him as he entered.
"I've got pie dough on my hands."

Duke took one look at Marnie and smiled. "And

flour on your nose." One moment he was standing smiling at Marnie, and the next he was kissing her.

Slowly, he raised his head and smiled at her in bemusement. "Do you always invite people into your house without knowing who they are?" he asked, scolding her gently.

Unmindful of the flour and sticky lard, Marnie pressed her hands to her breast and tried to contain her fluttering heart. "And do you always kiss your hostess as soon as you enter her home?"

"Only if she has sea-green eyes and sunset hair and flour on her nose." He continued to smile down at her, wondering at the overwhelming joy he felt because he was near her. "Seriously, Marnie, you should be more careful. I noticed that you don't even lock the door of the shanty."

"We don't lock anything up around here. This isn't Houston, or New York. No one is going to steal anything or harm us."

"Humor a cowboy from the big city, and let me lock up everything tonight, Marnie. I'm feeling fragile."

"There's nothing fragile about you," she said, looking him over slowly, deliberately, with admiration shining in her eyes.

He chuckled and shook his head, knowing she was teasing but feeling pleased as punch. "You're dead right about that, little Venus, and you know who's to blame." He shook his head again, trying to keep his mind on the reason he had stayed with

Marnie. "But I think I'll make the rounds and lock up anyway. Where are the keys?"

She pointed at the pegboard by the door. "Those are for the workshops, and you'll find the one for the shanty under the piece of driftwood I'm using for a doorstop. But I still think you're overreacting, Duke."

They both smiled at each other for a few sharing, caring moments before Duke left on his task. He might be overreacting, he thought, but he would rest easier if he knew he had done everything possible to keep Marnie safe.

Marnie turned from the counter to watch Duke as he entered the kitchen again. Clarence came in with him, and after giving a loud *meow*, jumped onto the couch and began licking a paw. Marnie barely spared Clarence a glance, her eyes riveted instead on Duke as he moved across the room with the sleek, smooth grace of a cheetah stalking its prey. She knew she was his prey, his willing prey, and she tilted her chin up as he lowered his head to capture her lips.

He could kiss her any time he wanted, Marnie thought, gripping his shoulders tightly as she returned his kiss. Because all he had to do was look at her, and she melted. All he had to do was smile at her, and she was filled with love. All he had to do was kiss her, and she was completely his.

When he finally raised his head, she gazed up at him, wanting to tell him that she loved him, but something in his eyes stopped her words. She swallowed hard, moistened her lips, and whispered instead, "I've got flour all over you."

"It doesn't matter," he said huskily. "As long as I can kiss you again."

His next kiss was hard, urgent, demanding, and she matched him demand for demand. She wanted him to kiss her, to make love with her, to be with her for the rest of his life.

Abruptly, he raised his head and stepped back from her, leaving her trembling. But he was also trembling, she noted, and his chest was heaving.

"I'm sorry, little Venus, but if I keep kissing you, you'll never get your dinner made." He brushed the flour off her nose with a finger that shook slightly. "So tell me, what can I do to help?"

The question was, what could she do to help, Marnie realized as she stared at Duke. This afternoon when they had made love, she had as much as told him she loved him, and he hadn't said one word about loving her. Perhaps if he admitted what was hurting him, he could get it out of his system. Then maybe he would fall in love with her . . . and want to marry her.

Perhaps she was dreaming, but she had to do something. She was no longer concerned only about Duke's happiness; her own happiness was at stake.

"You can ch-chop onions and c-celery and ch-chestnuts for the dressing," she stammered, her mind still reeling with thoughts. "The things are in the fridge."

She turned back to the counter and began rolling out crusts for the pumpkin pies, completely aware of every movement he made as he rummaged in the fridge, then brought the things to the sink. She moved along the counter to make room, but she was close enough that his elbow brushed her back, his hip her side. All she had to do was turn, and she would be in his arms.

"The sunset was beautiful tonight. I wish you had been there to share it with me," he said softly.

She turned her head slightly and studied him. "You're looking better, more relaxed."

"I'm feeling more relaxed than I've felt in years, more at peace with the world."

"I'm glad." But he still had a long way to go before he was at peace with himself, Marnie knew.

"This reminds me of my childhood," he said after he had finished washing the vegetables. "The kitchen was always the heart of our home. I don't know how Madre ever stood it with three boys and their friends underfoot, but she always made us feel welcome. We had some good times in that kitchen. Shared a lot of laughter and tears . . . and holiday preparations." He began chopping the onions, slowly, methodically.

"Didn't you go home for holidays after you were married?" Marnie asked as she fitted a crust into the fourth pie plate and fluted the edges.

"Not often. Usually, Karen had something else on the calendar." He chopped faster, harder. "She was very popular, and she gave terrific dinner parties."

Marnie glanced with concern at Duke's fingers and gave a sigh of relief that he was being careful despite his obvious agitation. But his agitation also told her where to start. "So you must have spent a lot of time in the kitchen helping her."

"We had a cook and housekeeper. For some reason Mrs. Webster stayed with me after the divorce, even though Karen wanted her to go with her."

"Maybe Mrs. Webster likes you better than Karen," Marnie said, and began pouring the pumpkin mixture into the shells.

Duke paused to look at her. "Karen wasn't an ogre, you know," he said, then resumed chopping. "She has lots of friends, belongs to all the in-clubs and organizations. When we were married, she was always attending some function or another."

"And you went with her?"

"Whenever I wasn't out of town or tied up in an unavoidable meeting . . . which was all too often, I'm afraid."

"And did you like the hectic pace?"

"At first. Then it became exhausting, especially when I was worried about the company going bankrupt. Sometimes I just wanted to go home and put up my feet. Or go sing with the boys, or go out to the ranch and ride."

His knife was flying now, and Marnie kept

glancing at him in concern as she placed the pies in the oven and a frying pan on the burner. "What did your family think of Karen?" she asked, adding some butter to the pan.

"Dad thought the sun rose and set on her, but Dare warned me against marrying her. I thought he was feeling a bit jaded about marriage because he'd just been left standing at the altar."

Duke paused, looked around, and realized he didn't have anything left to chop. Marnie moved to his side and smiled up at him as she transferred the pile of onions and celery into the frying pan. Her smile was tempered with relief, he noted, but her eyes still shone with concern, and he gazed at her thoughtfully. He had never told anyone about his life with Karen, had never uttered a word of complaint even after their divorce. Why was he talking so freely to Marnie? he wondered, when he hadn't even been as forthcoming with Dare, whom he had always felt close to.

"Dare didn't appear jaded to me," Marnie said. Removing the knife from Duke's hand, she replaced it with a spatula, then nudged him toward the stove.

Duke stared down at the mixture in the pan and gave it an unnecessary stir. "That's the funny thing, he isn't. And I think he's still in love with the gal."

Marnie took a deep breath, wondering if she was brave enough to carry on, wondering if she was ready to learn the answer to her next question. "Are you still in love with Karen?" she asked softly.

"No."

His answer was cold, hard, and flat; his eyes, cold, hard, and bleak as he gazed at her. She gazed back, relief sweeping through her body despite his desolate eyes.

"Then why don't you want to get married again?" she dared to ask.

"Because the divorce was mainly my fault." He turned his attention to stirring again. "I was a lousy husband."

He was carrying a load of guilt about their divorce, Marnie realized, but some of his previous comments made her wonder if he had ever been happy with Karen.

"Why was the divorce your fault?" she asked, determined to get at his true feelings.

"I didn't have the time or energy to put into the marriage."

"But if she hadn't been running around to so many parties, maybe you would have had more time for each other."

"Yeah, well, maybe." He shrugged an elegant shoulder. "But I couldn't provide her with the things she wanted most in life, no matter how hard I tried."

The pain in his voice tore at her, and for a moment she wondered if she had the strength to keep on digging into his past when it meant hurting him. "It sounds as if you gave her everything you humanly could."

"John gave her more."

"Some best friend he turned out to be," she said, feeling as angry with John as she was with Karen. Her anger was unreasonable, Marnie knew, but she couldn't help it. John and Karen had hurt the man she loved.

Duke glanced over his shoulder and frowned in puzzlement at the fierce expression on her face. "It wasn't really John's fault," Duke said. "He came to me before the divorce to assure me that he didn't deliberately go after Karen. And she didn't mean to fall in love with him. But I was away, and it had happened."

She gave an unladylike snort. "It sounds so civilized."

"Yeah." He prodded the onions and celery.

She deliberately prodded him. "I don't know how you can be so understanding."

The spatula flipped, and onions flew out of the pan. "Dammit, I'm not so understanding. I was devastated." He turned to stare at her, his eyes hooded, the muscle along his jawline jerking. "I've always believed marriage is a sacred trust, one a person doesn't betray or defile. Old-fashioned values, I guess, but I live by those values." He took a ragged breath. "Now, are you satisfied?"

Marnie came to him, placed her hands on his forearms, and carefully studied his face. "Yes, because you're being honest with yourself. And for the first time, I imagine."

Duke gave her a wry smile. "You're hard on a man's ego, Marnie."

"Any man who hasn't laughed or sung for four years and says his divorce hasn't affected him is lying to himself."

"Okay. Okay. So I felt betrayed, and I hurt," he admitted reluctantly, realizing even as he spoke that this was the first time he had ever allowed himself to express anger at Karen's betrayal.

Marnie watched him struggle to hide his pain and wished he weren't making the effort. "Why have you put up a front all these years?" she asked softly.

He closed his eyes and took a deep breath, and when he finally felt he had everything under control, he risked opening them again. "Because my father keeps taunting me about not being man enough to keep a wife happy, satisfied, and at home," he said, being as honest with Marnie as he could be, but knowing in his heart that she deserved more.

Rising on tiptoe, Marnie kissed him, then rocked back on her heels and gazed up at him earnestly. "You're father doesn't have a clue what he's talking about," she said staunchly. "Your lovemaking is out of this world, and any woman who would trade you for another man is out of her mind. I bet Karen is already regretting she divorced you."

He laughed huskily. "Now what are you trying to do? Put my ego back together?"

Marnie smiled, her eyes adoring him. "Have you seen her since the divorce?"

"I bump into them now and again," he said hoarsely, remembering the first time he had seen them after their baby had been born, and how it had taken every bit of self-control he'd possessed to ooh and aah over the beautiful little girl. And how he had gone around for weeks afterward, silently bleeding from the wounds in his heart.

His eyes were full of pain again, Marnie noted, and she felt despair settle around her like an overcast sky. She doubted she was making any progress in helping Duke to heal, but she still had to try. "And is she happy?"

"No," he said slowly, remembering with surprise how Karen had appeared to almost resent the baby and the attention John and everyone else had been paying to her. "I don't think she is."

"Then I doubt very much if anyone can make her happy," Marnie said, her voice full of conviction. "I believe that each of us is responsible for our own happiness. I can give you pleasant moments and maybe make you laugh, but I cannot make you feel happy. Only you can do that."

Shaking his head, he gave her a half-smile. "I disagree, Marnie. I have been happier these last few days than I've been in my entire life, and it's because I've been here with you."

She studied him intently. "But you still aren't completely happy."

"No," he admitted, knowing it was useless to lie. Marnie could read him like an open ledger.

Reaching out, he touched her cheek in a brief apology, then moved away from her. "And there is nothing you can do to help me."

His voice sounded so sad, so final, and so full of longing that it almost tore her apart. She didn't have the heart to hurt him anymore, but she wasn't going to give up either, Marnie decided. Thank goodness she had a few more days to—as he put it—work her magic. "Well, the least I can do is feed you before you mutiny and leave me with the rest of the preparations. How does broiled salmon sound?"

"Delicious."

The salmon was delicious, but not as delectable as their lovemaking afterward. Duke was still savoring it the next evening as he finished saying grace and began carving the large, golden-skinned turkey. Tradition, it seemed, dictated that he stand at the head of the table and carve while the other thirteen people seated around it watched. No, correction, he thought with a smile. Only twelve watched. Marnie, who was dressed in a beautiful hand-painted sunset-colored wraparound dress—which he had wrapped around her twice earlier that evening—and who was sitting at the foot of the table, kept her eyes averted.

So he carved, and Miss Mapleridge, who sat on his right, passed the plates along. Miss Mapleridge, an ex-librarian, had to be eighty if she was a day, but she flirted outrageously with him, and he flirted back while he wondered when he had last enjoyed himself so immensely at a dinner party. The people at this gathering were like none he'd ever met. Except for the black-haired, black-eyed Desiree, Marnie's friend and creator of her exotic clothes, they were the forgotten people, Duke suspected. Or people whom the islanders knew existed but considered too old, or odd, or too eccentric to invite into their homes. There was Flossie, a retired lady of the night, who wore feathers in her hat and around her shoulders; Larene, a romance writer, who at seventy was still looking for the man of her dreams; Hilda and Matilda, two sisters who had lived together for so long that one always finished the other's sentence; Bobby, a retarded man in his twenties who sat as close to Marnie as possible; Jeremy, a remittance man from England who couldn't keep his eyes off Larene; Tom, who couldn't keep his eyes off his wineglass; Peter, a one-armed old salt who had seen the wonders of the world, and Bartholomew, a handsome man in his forties who stared vacantly at things only he could see.

Each had a story to tell, tales of laughter as well as tears, and Duke suspected that Marnie was working deligently to make sure their stories had happy-ever-after endings.

Carving duties completed, Duke sank into his chair and gazed down the table at Marnie. She was carrying on three conversations at once, joking with Bobby while she helped Bartholomew cut up his food, and assuring Flossie that they would have a singsong after dinner. The folks would leave with bursting hearts as well as stomachs, and nourished souls as well as bodies. How many other "special friends" had come to Marnie's table over the years? he wondered. And would she continue to invite them to dinner when she had a family of her own?

Marnie looked up and smiled at him, her smile warm and tender and full of love, and Duke smiled back, knowing in that instant that he loved Marnie. He continued to gaze at her, and slowly the chatter and clinking of cutlery faded until there was just the two of them.

He didn't need to worry about Marnie not having enough love for him, Duke thought, or that it would last until he died. And the knowledge hurt his heart, because he knew he shouldn't even think about loving Marnie. It was too late, however; he'd begun to fall in love with her in the Garden of Eden, and everything he'd learned about her since they'd returned to the real world had made him love her more.

A tap on his left shoulder pulled his attention back to the present and Desiree, who was sitting beside him. "So, are you going to break her heart?" Desiree asked softly, giving him a cold once-over.

Duke stared at Desiree, realizing that her fragile, porcelin-doll appearance was deceiving. This woman would fight tooth and nail to protect the ones she loved.

"I hope not," he said hoarsely.

"You had better not, or you'll have me to answer to."

He looked away, wishing he could offer her more concrete reassurances but knowing he couldn't. Desiree was right. Marnie would be hurt when he left, and he could only hope she wouldn't be hurt too badly.

Hilda leaned forward, demanding his attention with a wave of her fork. "Mr. King, are you going . . ."

". . . to be staying around for long?" finished Matilda without missing a beat.

"Just for the weekend," he said, managing a smile for both women. "I'm afraid I have to leave on Monday."

"What a . . ."

". . . shame."

"We were sure . . ."

". . . you would enjoy living here."

"It's a beautiful spot," Duke assured them, thinking that even though Marnie had been willing to move to Houston to live with Jack, she would have had a hard time uprooting.

"You're from Texas, you say?" Peter asked.

"Yeah, Houston."

"I was there once, in 1918 or was it 1917?"

"It was '17," piped in Miss Mapleridge, who had obviously heard the story before, as had everyone else, because they all chipped in before he was finished.

Then Jeremy launched into a description of his home in England, and the stories continued while they consumed turkey and trimmings. Duke rose once and made the rounds of the table, filling wineglasses, and felt immeasurably pleased when Marnie casually rubbed his back as he bent over to fill her glass. His throat was still tight with emotion as he finished his pumpkin pie and whipped cream, then retired with the men to the living room. Marnie, he noticed, watched him go, even though she was stacking dishes and talking to Desiree.

"Be careful of him, luv, he's going to break your heart," Desiree said, following Marnie into the kitchen with a load of dishes.

Marnie set down her dishes on the counter and turned to face her friend. "I know, but there's nothing I can do about it."

"You could send him packing," Desiree said, vigorously scraping the scraps off a dinner plate.

"It's too late. I love him," Marnie said, then felt as if a great burden had been lifted because she had finally been able to tell someone about her love.

Desiree stopped scraping and stared at Marnie in dismay. "Oh no."

"Oh yes."

"But he's leaving on Monday."

"I knew that when I asked him to stay."

"Then why did you set yourself up for all this heartache?"

"Because he needed me," Marnie said, adding silently, *And I needed him*.

"You are such a pushover, Marnie," Desiree said, her black eyes full of concern. "You let everyone use you. Look at these people. Who else would fill their home with the rejects, the castoffs of society?"

"None of my friends are castoffs, especially you," Marnie said stoutly.

"Oh yes, I am, and you know it." Desiree wrapped her arm around Marnie and gave her a hug. "And I don't know what I would've done if it hadn't been for your friendship. Please, Marnie, take it from someone who knows. Don't give your heart to a man who doesn't want it."

"I believe Duke wants it, but for some reason he's unwilling to take it."

"And I think you're an incurable romantic." Desiree gave her another hug, then released her. "But I'll be here when you need me."

Entering the living room a few minutes later, Marnie felt her heart catch in her throat at the sight of Duke, standing tall and elegant next to the stone fireplace, talking to Jeremy. He cradled a brandy snifter in one hand, and the other was tucked casually into the pocket of black dress slacks that fit his slim pelvis and long legs to perfection. The midnight-blue shirt he wore was silk, she knew, because she helped him put it on—twice. Before and after they had made love at sunset.

Duke looked up and smiled at her, and suddenly Marnie knew that no matter what the future held in store, she would never regret asking Duke to stay. He looked happy, relaxed, and completely at home among her friends. Never once had he indicated by even the slightest raise of his eyebrow that he found anything strange about any of the people who had arrived for the party. To the contrary, he had treated each one with respect and genuine interest, had laughed at their corny jokes and had encouraged their stories. And had made her feel that this was the best Thanksgiving party she had ever given.

She knew she was feeling this way because, for the first time in her life, she felt as if she weren't alone. Her parents had always included her in their love, but they shared a special kind of closeness that she had begun to think she would never find for herself. But now that she had met Duke, she knew she could experience that closeness—if only he wouldn't keep pushing her away.

Forcing a smile to her lips, she led Flossie across the room to the old high-back piano.

"Gather 'round, everyone. It's time for our singsong," she called out cheerily, riffling through the worn songbook until she found what she wanted. "We'll start with 'Hail, Hail the Gang's All Here.'"

Flossie made the piano hop, but the gang had a

hard time staying on-key. Then Duke, who was standing at the end of the piano, began singing softly, unobtrusively. Soon everyone was following his lead, and Miss Mapleridge even went so far as to try harmonizing with him.

Caught up in the music and the good feeling that was flowing through the group, Marnie forgot herself and belted out the words to "Singin' in the Rain."

Amid groans and murmurs, Flossie quickly ended the song.

"Do us a favor, Marnie . . ."

". . . and don't sing anymore."

"Just turn the pages, that's a dear," Flossie pitched in.

Contrite, Marnie offered her apologies, then burst into laughter when Duke gave her a long, sorrowful look.

"She never could carry a tune, even in a bucket," Peter told him. "Can't imagine why she thought she could now."

"Sorry, everyone. Mum's the word. I promise."

She would never be able to sing duets out loud with Duke, Marnie thought regretfully, but then it didn't really matter. Because she would aways sing with him where it mattered—in her heart.

Somehow—and Marnie suspected that it was because of Flossie, who was a true romantic at heart—they began singing love songs, and finally the group fell silent and listened to Duke's beautiful voice. When he finished, the two sisters were dabbing unashamedly at the tears in their eyes, and Miss Mapleridge was looking at Peter, and Jeremy had his arms around Larene. The romantics were coming out of hiding, and Marnie knew exactly who was responsible. Duke with his sexy, heartwarming, soul-stirring voice.

It was an evening to remember, and no one wanted it to end, but finally the last song had been sung and the last tear shed. Larene was still wrapped up in Jeremy's arms, and Marnie quickly took Duke aside.

"Please offer to take the sisters home," she whispered. "Jeremy brought them, but I suspect he wants to be alone with Larene tonight. Of course, I could suggest they spend the night—"

"Oh, no, you don't," Duke said, laughing down at her. "I'll take them gladly. Just don't go inviting anyone else to stay. I want to be alone with you."

His smile was full of promise, and Marnie hugged the promise to herself as she hugged the others good night. Even Desiree's words of caution couldn't stop her glow of happiness, and she quickly began straightening up the house.

She could wait for Duke, she reasoned, but it would be much more fun to return to the Sea Shanty and set the stage for a night of loving. Now what could she do to surprise him? she wondered as she set off through the trees, a picnic basket full of goodies for later in her hand. Her mind was still busy with the possibilities when she opened the door of the Sea Shanty and came nose-to-nose with a gun.

EIGHT

Before she could think about turning tail and running, someone shoved her from behind, sending her farther into the room. A man caught her, steadied her, then released her, and she backed away to face her three captors. She didn't need the moonlight coming through the window to identify them. Why was her fantasy turning into a bad dream?

Sampson stepped into the room and closed the door behind him. "He ain't with her."

"What's g-going on here, Sampson?" she asked, her heart pounding in her throat. "If you b-boys wanted to come for dinner, all you had to do was ask."

"We looked in on you but decided to save the real party for later." Even in the moonlight she could see the leer Haigen gave her, and it made her wish

164

the bed were behind four solid walls and a double-locked door.

"Where in bloody hell did King go?" Booring demanded, waving the gun under her nose.

Instinctively, she batted the gun aside, then cringed, waiting for it to go off. When it didn't, she gamely tried to bluff. "He's left. So put away your gun and run along. There's no use hanging around."

Wheeling away from him, she walked on trembling legs to the table and placed the picnic basket on it.

Sampson jerked a thumb toward the bedroom. "He's coming back. He wouldn't go off and leave his clothes."

"Or a willing broad either," Haigen said, his voice sending a shiver of fear through her.

She pressed her hands to her chest, took a deep breath, and made up her mind that she wasn't going to let these bullies intimidate her. "What do you want him for?" she asked firmly.

"We was after you," Sampson said as he scratched his belly. "But when we seen King at the party tonight, we decided to kidnap you both."

"You're kidnapping me!"

Haigen swaggered toward her, and she edged around the table, hoping he wasn't getting any ideas about tying her up.

"We're going to make you pay for all the trouble you've put us through," he said, reaching into the picnic basket to retrieve a drumstick. He chomped off a strip of meat and chewed it hungrily. "We've been on the run from the cops for days; we might as well make it worthwhile."

"That's crazy talk!"

"Not so crazy. We've already called your old man and told—"

"You called Dad?" Marnie bit her lips in dismay. "Oh no!"

"And King's brother," Booring said, snatching a piece of breast meat out of the basket. "This time he bloody well didn't laugh at me when I demanded five million dollars. You're going to be our ticket to the good life in South America."

Marnie took another deep breath, then swallowed hard. "You won't get away with this," she said bravely.

"Who will stop us? You? Not likely, sweetheart," Haigen mumbled, his mouth full. He tossed the drumstick onto the table and reached for a roll, which he shoved into his mouth. "But thanks for giving us the idea. When we couldn't find King, we figured you'd slipped him out from under our noses. Then we heard you were missing and thought your boat might have sunk in the storm, so we called his brother and demanded a ransom. But then you had to go and spoil everything by turning up again, so we decided we'd kidnap you instead."

Marnie slumped into a chair and buried her head in her hands. It was all her fault she was in this mess and Duke was in danger. Had he known the men might be coming after her? she wondered. Was that the reason he hadn't gone home with Dare? Was that the reason he had insisted on locking up the place?

Zeus! She had to do something. She had to escape. Duke would be coming back anytime and would walk through the door right into a trap. But there was another way into the shanty, Marnie remembered suddenly, and rose to her feet. She was halfway across the room before Booring stopped her with a greasy hand on her arm.

"Where the bloody hell do you think you're going?"

She shook off his hand. "To the bathroom. Do you have any objections?"

"You're not going anywhere. Sit down."

"But I have—"

"Sit."

Ignoring him, she wheeled and walked into the kitchen, tore a paper towel from the roll, and wiped the grease off her arm. She felt like screaming in frustration. She felt like crying in fear. Forcing both feelings out of her mind, she tried to think of a way to warn Duke.

"You know, Duke is going to think it odd that I haven't turned on the lights," she said, hoping Duke would. She knew he had planned on a romantic evening, complete with candles and moonlight. Maybe if the lights were on, he'd realize something was wrong.

"She's right, Booring," Haigen mumbled, his mouth full.

"There ain't no curtains on the windows. We'd be sitting in a goldfish bowl."

"The glass is specially treated. You can't see in," Marnie said, wishing for the first time that the windows were normal. "Check it out if you don't believe me."

Without giving them a chance to object, she flipped on the kitchen light. Sampson lumbered for the door, while the other two hit the floor, Booring still holding his gun on her.

Sampson returned a minute later. Pulling a wicker chair out from the table, he turned it around and straddled it, then helped himself to a sweet potato. "Can't see nothing," he reported, grinning at the men as they rose to their feet and joined him.

"Well, now, this is much better," Marnie said, lying. She'd much prefer the moonlight, so she couldn't see the men clearly. They'd looked like bums the day she'd seen them at the resort, and after their three days on the run, even their mothers wouldn't invite them home. But in any other circumstances she'd be offering them the use of her shower and rooting out clean clothes for them. Shaking her head at her soft heart and even softer head, she turned to the counter. "I'm sure you boys would like a cup of coffee."

Booring started to object, but the others shut him up. "Well, okay. But someone had better keep an eye on the door. We don't want King catching us by surprise."

As she worked around the kitchen, Marnie desperately tried to think of another way to warn Duke. A phrase of a song flitted through her mind. She tried to ignore it, but it persisted, and suddenly she realized its significance. It was "The Wayward Wind." The song Duke had told her he'd sung when he'd been kidnapped. Maybe, if he heard her singing it, he would realize what was happening. It was a long shot, she knew, but it was the only thing she could think of. Now, if only she could pull it off.

She cleared her throat and began to sing, her voice squawking on the low notes and squeaking on the high ones.

"Bloody hell!"

"You call that singing?" Haigen objected.

Marnie stopped and gave a little laugh. "Sorry, boys. It's pretty bad, isn't it?"

"Bloody awful."

"I promised Duke I'd sing that song for him tonight. If he doesn't hear me practicing, he'll think something is wrong," Marnie said, and proceeded to do so as loudly as possible, all the while hoping and praying that Duke would hear her, realize what was happening, and go for help.

Duke hurried along the path, anxious to get back to Marnie. He had enjoyed escorting the sisters home, and had even flirted with Hilda. Hilda had flirted back, making him feel good that he had taken the extra time and trouble to sweet-talk the old lady.

Now he was ready to do some serious flirting with Marnie. He stopped at the edge of the trees, thinking about what he wanted to do with her, then frowned as he caught sight of the lighted kitchen. He had expected moonlight. Candles at the most. What was the matter? he wondered.

He heard Marnie singing and grinned. But the grin faded as he realized she was singing "The Wayward Wind."

Now why would she be singing that song? Especially when she knew it would bring back bad memories if he heard it. Fear slammed into his stomach as another thought occurred to him. Maybe she did want him to hear it. Maybe she was trying to tell him something.

Her voice squealed on the high notes, and Duke knew exactly what Marnie was trying to tell him. She had been kidnapped! Dammit all to hell! Why hadn't he been more careful? Why had he let the madness he felt when he was around Marnie affect his brain? Marnie was in danger, and it was all his fault.

Quickly, he considered his options. He could go back to the main house and phone for help. But the police wouldn't get within a hundred yards of the shanty without being detected because of those damn windows. And if there was a standoff, Marnie could get hurt. No, he'd have to rescue her himself. Sneak into the house and take them by surprise. But how?

He shivered as the answer came to him, and he tried desperately to think of another way. None came to mind, so keeping trees between himself and the shanty, Duke picked his way down to the beach, where he shed his boots and jacket, then waded into the water. It was frigid, and the sharp stones bit into his feet. Muttering curses, he waded deeper, until the water came up to his chest. A log floated nearby, and he ducked in behind it, pushing it in front of him as he swam toward the pier. The cold seeped into him, numbing his arms and legs. When he reached the pier, he clung to it, shivering in relief. Relief was short-lived as he realized what came next. He had to dive into the water and come up under the shanty. There was enough headspace, he knew; however, he would much rather take on a board-room full of corporate raiders than use Selina's route into the house.

A stray wave caught the log and thumped it into a piling. Above him on the pier, Clarence started meowing. Taking a deep breath, Duke sank into the black forbidding water.

"What the bloody hell was that?" Booring asked, jumping to his feet.

Marnie stopped singing and started praying in earnest. Oh, dear Lord, she hoped it wasn't Duke coming to rescue her. All she wanted was for him to go for help. But Duke wasn't the kind of man who would stand by or shirk danger. He was descending into the underworld to save her, as surely as all her make-believe stories had happy-ever-after endings.

"It's just Clarence," she said, her heart in her throat as she thought about what Duke was enduring for her sake. He didn't like the dark, and the underworld was as black as pitch and full of unseen dangers—not to mention Selina. And when he came up underneath, there would be very little headroom. Marnie's stomach clenched as she remembered how claustrophobic Duke got when he was in tight quarters.

"Who's Clarence?" Sampson demanded.

"He's my cat. Remember?"

Outside Clarence kept yowling insistently, while Marnie's heart echoed his wails. Why hadn't Duke phoned the sheriff for help? Why was he coming for her alone? Zeus, she had to do something to distract the men's attention.

"I'd better let Clarence in," she said loudly. "Duke would think it odd if he came along and found Clarence outside meowing."

"He sounds better than your caterwauling."

Marnie shoved at a chair, knocking it clattering across the floor. "Just because you've kidnapped me doesn't give you the right to insult me. I'll have you know I'm a good singer."

The men laughed and hooted, and Marnie walked toward the door, stomping as loudly as her high heels would allow. Lord, if Duke was really down there, she hoped he was coming up through the hatch about now. She couldn't think of another excuse to make noise.

"Well, boys, aren't you afraid I'm going to escape?" she called as she swung open the door. "Just kidding," she hastened to assure the three startled men who had jumped to their feet and were now staring at her.

A fourth man—a dripping-wet man—was standing in the doorway of the bathroom, staring at her too. Hiding her relief, she leaned over to pick up Clarence, hiking up her skirt, showing as much leg as possible. Still crouched, she swung around and threw Clarence straight at Booring. The gun he held went sailing, and for the next few minutes, pandemonium reigned. Haigen toppled over like a rotten tree, felled by Duke's karate chop to the back of his neck. Duke's flying foot slammed into Sampson's stomach, and the big man moaned as he held his midsection. And Marnie had the supreme pleasure of banging the driftwood doorstop over Booring's head.

"Oh, Duke, Duke, I was so frightened for you," Marnie said, flinging her arms around Duke and pressing against his cold, wet body.

Duke hugged her close with one arm and kept the gun trained on the groaning, swearing men. "Not as frightened as I was about you," he said, contenting himself with a kiss on the top of her head when what he really wanted to do was search every inch of her body to make sure she hadn't been harmed. "Are you all right? Did they hurt you?"

"I'm fine," she murmured.

She was shaking, however, and he hugged her even closer. "Thank God."

Belatedly remembering the sodden state of his clothes, Duke tried to draw back, but she wouldn't let him go. Standing on her toes, she kissed him, and it took every ounce of Duke's willpower to keep his eyes and mind on the men. When they began stirring, he reluctantly eased Marnie away from him.

"I think you'd better phone the police," he said. "The sooner we get rid of these deadbeats, the better."

Marnie drew in a sigh, then turned toward the kitchen just as Sheriff Morsely stepped through the open door, his gun drawn.

"No need, Marnie, your father has been burning up the lines," Morsely said, then waved his arm to summon Deputy Parry into the room. A few minutes later they were leaving again with the subdued, handcuffed men in tow.

"I think you'd better call your father, Marnie," the sheriff told her as he headed out the door. "He's real worried about you. And your brother wants to know what the hell's going on, King, so you'd better contact him too."

❖———————❖

Much later—after the MacBrides, the Kings, and Clarence had been reassured, and after Duke and Marnie had shared a long, hot shower—Marnie lay against Duke's shoulder and gazed at him as he stroked her hair. He was propped up against the scalloped headboard, a sheet covering him from the waist down, leaving his lean, muscular torso exposed to the moonlight and her admiring eyes.

"Are you warm enough?" she asked, running a hand along his rib cage, checking once again that he was all right.

"After the workout you just put me through, how could I be cold?" he asked, and her cheeks flushed as she thought about their lovemaking.

"You could be suffering from hypothermia," she said, although he had proved very capably that he wasn't. "That water was freezing."

"Tell me about it!" He smiled down at her as he toyed with a lock of hair that was curled over her breasts. "Hey, why didn't you warm me up that way the first time I took a dip?" he teased.

"Because I didn't know you," she said primly.

"And you know me now, after only three short days?"

She pressed a kiss against his chest, right above his heart. "I know you're happy; you keep smiling."

"You're right. I can't remember when I've had such an enjoyable day." He nuzzled her temple, then shivered. "Except the kidnapping, of course. The thought of your being in the hands of those men makes my skin crawl."

His voice was filled with concern, and she basked in it, just as she had basked in the warmth of his loving a few minutes earlier. But she didn't want Duke to keep worrying about her, so she teased gently, "You can't fool me, Duke. You enjoyed the kidnapping, especially the rescue part. It gave you a chance to have a grand adventure."

He cupped her breast in his hand. "I admit there's something satisfying about seeing that justice is done," he said, forcing himself to lighten up. "And don't tell me that you didn't have a ball, Marnie. You were something else, warning me with your singing—although I still don't understand why they didn't turn themselves in when you started." He laughed as she punched him in the stomach. "Really, Marnie, that was a stroke of genius. Then the way you distracted them—although I wasn't too happy about the amount of leg you were showing. Not that they aren't beautiful," he hastened to assure her, and trailed his fingers over her hip and down her leg . . . then up the inside of her thigh.

"Duke!"

"And the way you threw Clarence at Booring, and then hit him with that log. Remind me not to get too close to you when you're in a temper," he said, his fingers moving higher.

"Well, I should be mad at you, the way you

came charging to the rescue yourself. You should have called for reinforcements. You could've gotten hung up on something under the pier and drowned or—Duke!" she exclaimed, all thoughts scattering as his fingers eased into her soft, sensitive folds.

He cupped her, feeling her heat against his hand, feeling his own body surge in response. "I would have gone through worse to keep you safe."

His words penetrated the wonderful feeling that had begun to build inside her, and brought her back to reality. Reaching down, she pulled his hand up to her waist. "That's why you stayed behind, isn't it, Duke?" she asked. "You were afraid those men were going to come after me."

Undeterred by her action, he moved his hand back to her breast and began caressing her. "Dare mentioned they'd made some threats when they realized their first ransom demand wasn't going to work, but it wasn't anything we could take to the police. I didn't feel right about leaving you here by yourself."

She closed her eyes, struggling to keep the tears at bay as the significance of his comments sank home. Duke had remained behind because he'd felt an obligation toward her, not because he loved her. And if he had fallen in love with her since then, surely he would have told her after he had rescued her. But he hadn't, so reaching deep, Marnie found the strength to manage a brief, lighthearted laugh.

"Besides, you wanted to see if you could make my dream come true."

If it were in his power, he would make all her dreams come true, Duke thought, wondering when the anguish in his soul would subside—if ever. He started to say something, then paused, afraid that if he uttered a single word, he'd be telling her that he loved her. And he couldn't do that.

"You don't have to stay any longer," she whispered when he remained silent.

"I promised your father I would wait until he and your mother got back."

Marnie gave a brief prayer of thanks that her parents had agreed to wait until Sunday to return. At least she would have a few more days with Duke. A few more days to win his love, because she wasn't going to cut bait and give up on him yet. "So you did, Duke. Thank you." She took a deep breath, determined to dispel her sadness. "Your mother sounded very nice on the phone. And your grandmother was a real dear."

"You'd like them," he said, certain they would love Marnie. If only things were different, and he could take Marnie home. They would welcome her with open arms, because they'd take one look at him and know how much he loved her.

"I'm sorry we had to ruin their Thanksgiving. It's such a special day, isn't it?"

Duke rolled over, his hard, naked body atop

hers. Bracing himself on his elbows, he cupped her face in his hands and gazed into her eyes. "That was what I was talking about earlier, Marnie. How very special this day has been. How much I enjoyed helping you prepare the meal. How much I enjoyed meeting your friends, singing with them." He pressed a soft kiss against her lips. "And the reason everything was so special was because of you, little Venus. Because of the love you give so freely." Arching his back, he bent to take her nipple in his mouth. "It's time someone gave some loving to you," he murmured, and proceeded to do so slowly and thoroughly.

His warm, firm lips adored her breast, and his hot, moist mouth suckled it until her whole body was throbbing with the need for release. And he had only begun, Marnie thought. His hand sought her, held her still, and she gave a low moan, partly in protest, partly in need.

His lips moved on to her other breast, lavishing it with just as much tender, loving care, and all the while Marnie made soft little crying sounds in the back of her throat. Her cries turned to mews of pleasure as he burned a path of openmouthed kisses down her tummy and into the delta of hair below. She felt the warmth of his breath, then the touch of his lips, and sobbed out his name again and again as he generously loved her.

She had never known this kind of loving before,

had never felt so adored. And she felt so proud and so humble that Duke would want to love her in this way. Then all thoughts vanished as a ripple of rapture swept through her, followed by one tidal wave after another until her whole body was flooded with the ecstasy of Duke's loving. She cried out as she reached the crest and gripped his shoulders. He held her, supporting her as the pleasure washed through her, then slowly ebbed away.

Finally, Duke raised his head and gazed down at her, his eyes shining like moonlight. "You are so beautiful, little Venus, and you make me crazy with all your moans and sighs and cries."

"And you made me crazy with your loving," she said, her voice a breathy whisper. "I've never been loved that way before."

The smile he gave her was filled with pleasure. "I'm glad I was your first," he said, before lowering his head to kiss her.

She kissed him back, thoroughly, deeply. She heard a growl rumble in his chest, felt the hard ridge of his manhood as it pressed against her, and marveled at his self-control. Her hands sought him, found him, and caressed him, and she smiled in satisfaction as he growled again and raised his head.

"You're asking for trouble, little Venus."

"I'm asking for loving," she said, smiling up at him as she gave him a little push. "And this time it's my turn to love you."

"I guess a mere mortal has no chance when the goddess of love wields her powers," Duke said, rolling off her to lie flat on his back, his arms stretched over his head. "So, I'm all yours, little Venus. Love me."

NINE

Duke hadn't expected she would want to love him the way he had just loved her, and it almost shattered his soul when she knelt beside him and proceeded to do so. Loving him so freely, so generously, so adoringly, that he almost died from the sheer torture of it all. No other woman had loved him so unselfishly, he realized, before all thought fled. Gripping the edges of the bed, he gave himself up to the pleasure of being loved by Marnie.

And when he could no longer stand the tantalizing flicks of her tongue and the lavish touch of her lips, he reached down and raised her head from him. She gazed at him, her eyes shining, and smiled as she tried to lower her head again. But he held her.

"No, little love, I want to be in you now. I want to feel you throbbing around me."

He half rose, but she pushed him down. Holding

him there with a sultry smile, she straddled him, and slowly, ever so slowly, inch by silken inch, lowered herself onto his pulsing shaft.

When she had finally taken all of him, she sat on him, wiggling closer. Her extra weight pushed him down against the cushion of water, which bounced him back, and she gasped, then smiled in pleasure as he reached higher inside her. Deliberately, she swayed against him, setting up a slow rocking movement that made him weak from wanting her.

But he held off and watched her ride him, enjoying the way her eyes grew wider with each thrust, loving the way she moistened her lips, captivated by the way she crooned every time he thrust into her.

She was Venus, Duke thought, the picture of Marnie riding him in the moonlight taking his breath away. Moonlight set fire to her hair, which tumbled over her shoulders to curl around her breasts. Moonlight also dappled her skin with pearls, the same color as the fan-shaped footboard that curled up behind her like a giant seashell. It was a vision he would carry to his grave, he knew. Marnie in the moonlight. Venus rising out of the sea to ride the waves of love.

Although he would never say the words, he would love her forever. And because he couldn't say the words, he loved her the only way he could, with his eyes, his body, and his heart.

When she called out in joy, he joined her. When

she collapsed into his arms, he held her. And when she finally fell asleep, he loved her with all the aching loneliness of his soul.

Duke lay awake for the rest of the night, holding Marnie in his arms and fighting the urge to tell her that he loved her. But he couldn't, he knew, because he couldn't give her all the things she wanted in life. So he held her and dreamed about what might have been if the real world were perfect, or barring that, if they could spend the rest of their lives in Marnie's Land West of the Sun and East of the Moon.

In her fantasyland he could marry Marnie, and they could have all the children she wanted, maybe even adopt a few more. Marnie would teach them to sail, and he would teach them to sing, and their house—a salvaged barn if that was what Marnie wanted—would be full of laughter and love, with plenty of room for their families to come and visit, along with all the forgotten people Marnie was sure to bring home.

They'd have to have an orphanage, too, and Marnie and the children would nurse the animals back to health. Because there was no doubt in his mind that their children would be just as warm and loving as their mother . . . and that he'd be the happiest man in the world.

But that had been a fantasyland, Duke reminded himself early the next morning as he followed Marnie into the fenced orphanage. This was the real world, where a man like him dared not to dream.

"I think I'll let Blue Boy go today," Marnie said after they had finished feeding the heron. "There is nothing more I can do for him."

Duke stood back as Marnie gently herded the bird out of the holding cage into the main yard. The heron remained proud and aloof from Marnie, Duke noted, and didn't seem to appreciate her tender care. Of course, it was only a wild bird, and Marnie had made no effort to tame it, but she still must feel disappointment. Marnie must also be disappointed because he hadn't responded to her TLC, Duke thought, and wished again he could tell her his true feelings.

Pushing the thought aside, Duke watched the bird stroll hesitantly around the yard. "He doesn't want to go."

"We'll just leave him alone, and he'll go in his own time," Marnie said, coming over to loop her arm through Duke's. "Meanwhile, let's feed the gulls."

Duke kept an eye on the heron, while Marnie entered the cage and began filling the old bathtub with water. Blue Boy, it appeared, wasn't going anywhere. Despite his apparent indifference toward Marnie, he obviously knew a good thing. And he didn't blame the bird, Duke decided, because he, too, didn't want to leave. If only there were a way . . .

Marnie came to join him. "Have you ever considered adopting a child, Marnie?" he asked.

"Someday I would like to," she said, smiling up

at him. "But looking after these orphans and letting them go has made me realize how much I want to have a child—preferably more than one—of my own. I want to know that when I send my children off into the world, I'll be sending part of me that will survive into the next generation and the next. You, of all people, should understand what I'm talking about. After all, you're the oldest son of the oldest son."

"Yeah, I know what you mean," Duke said hoarsely, then turned away to look at the water while a foghorn moaned deep in his soul.

"Sometimes when I'm working with wood or walking in the forest, I hear voices talking to me, and I know that they must belong to my ancestors," Marnie continued softly. "I would like to believe that my children's children's children will hear my voice when they are traveling the galaxies."

She heard a ragged sigh and stared at Duke in concern. "Duke, are you all right?" she asked, moving forward to place a hand on his arm.

Half turning, he wrapped his arms around her and rested his chin on the top of her head. "Hold on to your dream," he said, his voice husky with suppressed emotion. "You, more than any woman I know, deserve to have children of your own."

She nestled her cheek against his sweater right above his heart. "Maybe I'm too much of a romantic. Maybe I should start looking at things realistically. The chances of my having a child are getting more remote with each passing day."

She sounded utterly discouraged, and Duke hugged her, wanting to assure her that everything would work out all right. And although it hurt like hell, for her sake he forced himself to say, "You could marry Gil."

The bitter taste of disappointment burned her throat, and for a moment Marnie couldn't speak. "I told you before that I won't marry a man who doesn't love me. Gil doesn't love me; he needs me."

"And I'm positive that Gil loves you," Duke said, each word piercing him like a dagger. "He just hasn't gotten around to telling you yet."

"Well, it doesn't matter because I—"

"Look," Duke interrupted, and turned Marnie around in his arms. "Blue Boy has decided to leave."

They watched as the big bird flapped its long wings and rose awkwardly into the air. It flew out toward the sea, then turned and glided back over the orphanage. Duke could've sworn it dipped its wings in a salute to Marnie before flying off.

"Look at that! He's thanking you, Marnie."

Marnie looked up at Duke, tears shining in her eyes. "Yeah, I guess he is."

"No wonder. He has a lot to be thankful for," Duke said, gazing down at Marnie for long moments, drinking in her beauty and goodness and storing them in his heart. Slowly, he bent his head and brushed a soft kiss against her lips. "And so do I. Thank you, Marnie, from the bottom of my heart."

Raising his head, he gave her a sad smile, then turned away. "If you don't get the rest of the orphans fed soon, your help is going to drop dead from hunger."

The pain in his eyes shook Marnie to the core. She followed Duke into the barn, torn between the desire to confront him and the need to protect herself. Because if she did ask him how he felt about her, she was afraid his answer would destroy the fantasy world she'd been living in. For despite all the openings she'd given him, he hadn't once said he loved her. In fact, he was virtually shoving her into Gil's arms—a sure sign that he didn't want anything from her except a brief affair.

And yet, every time he held her, every time he made love to her, his body told her how much he wanted her. If only she could find a way to soothe the pain from his eyes, perhaps his heart would want her too.

As she made the rounds of the cages, she kept looking at Duke, who was feeding Delight. The fawn had snuggled up as close as she could get to Duke, and he kept petting her as he held the bottle.

"You handle that bottle as if you've been doing it for ages," Marnie said, her heart going all soft and mushy again at the sight of the handsome man and the tiny fawn. "You'd make a good father."

He glanced up at her, his eyes hooded. "You think so?"

"I know so." He looked so endearing that she

wanted to go to him and give him a hug. She sent him a warm smile instead. "Why didn't you and Karen have children? Didn't you want them?"

"Yes, we wanted children," he said, his voice so low, she could barely hear him. "That was one of the reasons I married Karen. She was as crazy about them as I was. But it didn't work out."

"I'm sorry," Marnie offered. Duke was such a sexy, virile man, it was a shame Karen hadn't been able to give him the children he wanted. He must have been terribly disappointed, Marnie thought, especially when having a son meant so much to him.

Duke continued to pet Delight as he thought about how disappointed he had been when a year, then two, had passed, and Karen hadn't become pregnant. He had even swallowed his pride and suggested they take some fertility tests, but she had adamantly refused, saying she didn't want a doctor poking around in their private lives. When he had pressed, she had become hysterical, yelling that she wasn't to blame. And then she had gone out and proved she wasn't.

"Yeah, well, this is the real world, Marnie," Duke said softly. "Where people don't always get what they want." Giving Delight a final pat, he rose to his feet and stood, smiling wryly at the baby bottle in his hand. "But is there any chance of my getting breakfast now? I'm starved."

They had just entered the kitchen of the main

house when the phone began ringing. Marnie answered it.

"Hello. Oh, hi, Desiree. We are?" She cupped the mouthpiece and told Duke, "We're on the morning news." Speaking into the phone again, she reassured Desiree, "No, we're fine. No, you don't need to come out and hold my hand, but thanks." After a few more words of reassurance, she hung up.

The phone rang again; this time it was the Channel 5 crew. The next call was for Duke from an investor worried about his money.

"Damn. I'd better start doing some damage control," Duke said. "If you can hold breakfast awhile, I'll make my calls from the living room."

He made his calls, then took a quick trip to the bathroom to wash his hands. The phone was ringing for the fifth time when he reentered the living room. He picked it up just as Marnie called, "I've got it, Duke."

Her greeting came on the line, and before Duke could speak, another voice answered. "Marnie, Marnie, honey. What's going on up there? I saw the news. Are you all right?"

"I'm fine, Gil. Honest," Marnie said. "If I'd known the media had gotten hold of the story, I would've phoned you to tell you not to worry."

"Not worry, when the woman I love is held for ransom!" Gil said, his voice full of concern. "I'm coming home on the afternoon ferry, and we'll get married as soon as possible. I don't want you living alone—"

Duke silently hung up the phone and stared at it blindly. Gil had finally said the words Marnie had been waiting to hear. Now she could have everything she wanted. A man who loved her as well as needed her . . . and children.

And he had to get the hell out of her life before he ruined her chance for happiness. Had to be long gone before Gil arrived home. Lord, he should be shot for making a move on Marnie when he'd known she was almost promised to another man. It had been he who had pressured Marnie into making love. He who had asked her to help him. And she had given of herself so freely . . . her laughter, her body, and her TLC.

Silently, Duke rose, crossed the room, and glanced cautiously into the kitchen. Discovering that Marnie had finished her conversation, he went back to the desk and made another call.

"Well, has the damage been controlled?" Marnie asked when he walked into the kitchen a few minutes later.

She looked so adorable standing there with flour on her chin that it was all he could do to keep from crossing the floor and kissing her. Instead, he sat down at the table. "I'm afraid I've got to go home," he said tersely. "The helicopter will be here in about an hour."

Marnie dropped the rolling pin on top of the

biscuit dough and stared at Duke in dismay. "What? So soon? I thought you were going to stay until Mom and Dad got back."

"I'm sorry, it can't be helped. If you feel uneasy about being here all alone, I'll arrange for a guard. The sheriff promised he'd hold the men in custody at least until Monday, and a restraining order will be issued to keep them off the island."

She picked up the rolling pin and began rolling the dough—hard. "A guard isn't necessary. Gil has insisted on coming home," she told Duke. Trying not to think, trying not to feel, she babbled on. "I feel so bad that he's cutting his holiday short, but he won't take no for an answer. At least he's going to leave the children with his folks, so their holiday won't be ruined."

"Then I'm sure glad I'm leaving," Duke said, continuing to brazen it out. The last thing he wanted now was for Marnie to guess he had overheard her conversation with Gil. "I'm sorry, Marnie. I should've realized that if I stayed with you, I would put you in a compromising situation." He rose to his feet and began pacing. "Hell, half the island came to dinner, then the other half showed up after the kidnapping. And then we talked to your parents and—" He stopped pacing and gazed at Marnie's back and bowed shoulders. "I'm sorry. I hope I haven't ruined things between you and Gil."

Marnie stared down at the dough, which was now as flat as her dreams. "Duke, I told you before, there was nothing to ruin. I hadn't made any promises to Gil."

"But you should marry him," Duke said earnestly. Then, taking a deep breath, he coolly, calmy, told her all the reasons why. "Gil obviously loves you and will make you a good husband. He'll give you the things you want . . . children, your chance at immortality. He'll have time to be with you, to be there for you when you need him. And you won't even have to leave home, much less the beautiful island you love."

Suddenly, Marnie had had enough. She wheeled away from the counter and walked toward Duke. "You've got my life all planned out, haven't you?" she asked, waving the rolling pin at him.

He took a step backward. "Ah, yeah. I guess so."

"Well there's one minor hitch in this business scenario you're concocting." She waved the pin at him again, then threw it onto the counter, where it bounced and fell to the floor. "How can I marry Gil when I love you?"

Duke stared at her in dismay as her words tolled a bell in his soul. Oh, Lord, she loved him. He had never meant for that to happen. Had never meant to hurt Marnie. "You love me?" he asked, feeling sick and ashamed and so very, very sorry.

"Yes," she said, tilting her head.

"You can't fall in love with me."

"It's too late, Duke. I think I've loved you forever."

She looked so brave, so determined, that it took every ounce of Duke's self-control to keep from telling her that he loved her in return. "But you love everyone and everything," he said instead, struggling to find the words. "You love each and every one of the guests who came for dinner. You love Clarence and all your orphans. You even love broken boats and abandoned sheds."

She looked up at him, her green eyes shining like emeralds. "Yes, I love them, but you know as well as I do that my love for you is a different kind of love—one reserved for the man of my dreams."

"I can't be that man, Marnie," he said, forcing the words past vocal cords so tight, he could barely speak. "I . . . told you at the very beginning that I wouldn't marry you, and I still can't."

"Why not?" she asked, reaching out to clasp his arm with her strong hand.

Every muscle in Duke's body ached with the need to take her in his arms, but somehow he held himself rigid as he gazed at her, his eyes hooded. "Because I couldn't make you happy, Marnie. I went through hell for you last night, but it would be heaven compared to the hell I'd put us both through if I married you." With gentle fingers he removed her hand from his arm, then stepped away. "So forget about me and get on with your life. Find someone else to make your dreams come true."

Marnie stared at him in bewilderment. "But my

dreams aren't any different from yours," she cried out. "I want a husband who loves me, and children. You want a grandson to visit your grave. Why won't you help me make them come true?" She would have said more, but he made a choking sound and closed his eyes tightly. When he opened them again, they were unguarded, vulnerable, and what she saw in them stopped the words in her throat.

"Please, Marnie, if you love me, don't ask me to explain," he whispered. "Please leave me with my pride. It's all I've got left."

Then he turned and fled. And because she had seen the soul-deep pain in his eyes, she let him go.

Standing at the window, she stared blindly through a film of tears and waited until the helicopter arrived. Waited while she watched Duke climb aboard, without a farewell glance or wave. Waited until the helicopter rose into the air, and without even dipping its tail in a salute, disappeared out of sight.

Turning from the window, she bent to pick up Clarence, who had been sitting quietly at her feet, and carried him into the living room. She sank onto the couch and finally let the tears flow unchecked as the agonizing reality hit home.

Duke had flown out of her life and had taken her dreams with him.

All along she had clung to the hope that he would fall in love with her, marry her, and make her dreams come true.

"But Duke was right," she told Clarence as he licked the tears from her cheeks. "This is the real world, and dreams don't always come true."

In all her make-believe worlds, the pirate had always married the woman he kidnapped, the king had always made Cinderella his queen, and everyone had always lived happily ever after.

Never had the knight in shining armor run away.

Finally, Clarence remembered he was a cat, and with a soft *meow* wiggled out of her arms. Brushing the tears from her face with the backs of her hands, Marnie rose and walked into the kitchen, where she picked the rolling pin off the floor, then methodically scraped the biscuit dough off the counter and threw it into the trash. After washing her hands and face, she walked—toes dragging, head bowed—down to her Sea Shanty.

Opening the door, she stepped inside and was met by an overwhelming sense that Duke was still there. He had taken all his belongings, she noted, but she could feel his presence everywhere. She could see him sitting across the table laughing at her, standing in the tiny shower holding her, and lying in the bed loving her. How could she continue to live there without him?

Her vision blurred as more tears welled up. With a sob she threw herself on the bed and let memories take over. Memories of Duke the serious-minded businessman, playing make-believe in the fog. Of

Duke the swashbuckling pirate, swinging on the mast and singing love songs to her. Of Duke the king dressed in his white robes, lounging on the cushions . . . then making her his queen.

Memories eventually gave way to despair. She had done it again. She had fallen in love with a man who needed her but did not love her. Never once had Duke said he loved her. Not even in the throes of passion, when men were apt to say anything to make a woman feel good.

Duke had loved her with his body, but he hadn't loved her with his heart and soul.

If only she had had more time to work her magic. If only he had told her what hurt him so badly. If only he weren't such a proud, stubborn man.

Well, if pride was more important to him than she was, so be it, Marnie decided, resolutely pushing herself off the bed and drying her eyes. For a moment she struggled with the urge to hop on the first plane to Texas and confront him once more. But she couldn't do that. Not after the way he had begged her to let him go. She let her orphans go without making a fuss—the least she could do was let Duke go too.

So, that was that, she told herself sternly. She would stop feeling sorry for herself and get on with her life. Which meant she would have to start by talking to Gil. Suddenly remembering that he was due in on the midafternoon ferry, she glanced at her watch, then bolted for the bathroom. No way was she about to let Gil see how upset she was. Not that she wouldn't shed more tears when she was talking to him, she knew. Because she was going to have to tell him she couldn't marry him.

"Why won't you marry me?" Gil asked her an hour later, and Marnie almost burst into tears again. Hadn't she asked the same question of Duke that morning? Hadn't she been as confused and bewildered as Gil was right now?

"Because I don't love you the way you deserve to be loved," she said, reaching out to take his hand. She stared at his callused palm, blinking hard, then looked up into his sky-blue eyes. "I love you as a good friend, as the brother I never had, but I don't love you the way a wife should love her husband."

He stared down at her, his weather-beaten face full of understanding. "I know you're still getting over Jack, but I'm sure you can learn to love me, given time."

"No, Gil, I can't. I wish with all my heart that I could love you, could marry you, could be the mother to your children, but I can't." She squeezed his hand and gazed up at him earnestly. "I'm sorry if I've hurt you, but it's for the best. You'll see. Because I really don't think you love me either, the way I deserve to be loved. You love me like a sister and a friend, but you don't love me the way you loved Sonja."

He bowed his head, considering her words.

"You're probably right, but we could make it work."

"No, we couldn't. We'd make each other miserable." She squeezed his hand once more, then released it. "Don't sell yourself short, Gil. Hold out until you find someone you love so much, you would die for her, and who feels the same way about you."

"Something's happened to you since you sailed off to the resort, hasn't it?"

"I guess I've finally grown up. Faced facts. Faced reality."

Gil's eyes grew thoughtful. "And found someone else to love," he guessed. "Is it that fellow they mentioned on the news? King?"

Marnie hesitated, then answered honestly, "Yes."

"But he doesn't love you?"

"No. At least I don't think so," she said, suddenly beginning to wonder if Duke might love her after all. Hadn't he risked his life for her when it hadn't been necessary? All Duke had to do was call the police and wait for them to rescue her, but he hadn't. He had descended into hell for her. Because he loved her?

The question remained with her long after she had finally convinced Gil that she would be all right, long after he had left for his home. Long after she had wandered down to the docks and found the envelope Duke had left for her aboard the *Homeward Bound*.

The envelope contained a check for a sum of

money that made her gasp, and a note with the words
For your dream, Marnie. May it come true.

"Yes, it will come true, Duke," she whispered.
"Thanks to you."

But it wasn't until forty-five long days and forty-five achingly lonely nights had passed that she realized Duke had made another dream come true.

She was pregnant.

TEN

Duke turned from the window, watching as Dare ambled into his office, settled his lanky frame into one of the big chairs in front of his desk, and crossed his booted feet.

"How's the Baron taking it?" Duke asked, raking a weary hand through his disheveled hair.

"Better than you, by the look of things. That was a humdinger of a board meeting, and I, for one, am glad it's over."

Moving to the desk, Duke hiked up his slacks and slid onto the corner. "Thanks for backing me."

"I should've backed you years ago, the first time the Baron landed us in a mess, but . . ."

Duke waved his hand. "No apologies necessary."

"Anyway, I'm glad you're the official president

of this company. Now I can go back to fighting fires in Kuwait and not have to worry about King Oil."

"I appreciate your flying home for the board meeting," Duke said, and leaned forward to give emphasis to his request. "Why don't you quit running after danger and help me run the company? There's more than enough work to keep you busy, and I promise to stay out of your hair."

"Maybe I'll come home and take over the ranch, but later, after we make sure the fires are out."

"Well, make damn good and sure you keep your head up. I don't want to have to go over there and bring your body home."

"Now don't ya be worryin' 'bout me, Big Brother," Dare drawled, his big body looking so relaxed that it would take a load of dynamite to move it. "I lead a charmed life."

The door opened, and Devlin, the youngest member of the King family, strode in and sat down on the other chair. "Are you all right, Duke?" he asked.

"I'll survive. Thanks for your support," Duke said, smiling at the handsome congressman.

"You came to Washington when I needed you. It's the least I could do."

"Yeah, well, thanks anyway."

Dev leaned forward, ready to do battle. "I don't know why you didn't haul off and slug the old man after the things he said about you."

Duke shrugged his shoulders, but a muscle

jerked along the side of his jaw. "The Baron has said them before. Worse, in fact."

"But to ask the board how they could have confidence in your ability to run the company when you hadn't been able to handle your own wife was unforgivable."

"Hey, now. Don't go off half-cocked on my account," Duke said, trying to take the wind out of Dev's sails before he did something rash. "You've settled your own differences with the Baron, don't take up my cause."

"Well, someone should."

"There is one thing you could do to help," Duke suggested with a half-smile, thinking of the beautiful woman Dev had recently become engaged to.

"Yeah, what?"

Duke's smile broadened. "You and Kristi could get busy and produce a child. That would get Mother and Grandmother off my back."

Dev laughed. "Give us time. We aren't married yet. And you know how strict Madre is about getting first things first."

"So, when are y'all getting hitched?" Dare asked.

"Soon, real soon." Dev rose to his feet. "And speaking of priorities, I have to get back to Washington tonight. Kristi's flying in from Alaska, and I want to be there to meet her. Take care, Dare," he said, slapping Dare's shoulder. Then he turned to take Duke's hand. "And you take care too, Duke. I sure am glad you're running the company. But what makes me even happier is seeing you smile again. Keep it up."

Duke managed to keep smiling until Dev had breezed out of the room.

"Ah, true love. Isn't it wonderful?" Dare said in a soft drawl.

"Yeah."

"So what happened between you and Marnie? I thought you'd found your true love this time."

"It wouldn't work out," Duke said, wishing for the millionth time he could find a way to make it work. Wishing he could fly back to the West Coast and ask Marnie to marry him. But he was probably too late, he told himself. Gil had probably married her by now.

"Why not?"

Duke glared at his brother. "Drop it, Dare."

Dare settled his shoulders deeper into the back of the chair, tented his hands on his flat stomach, and considered Duke thoughtfully. "Okay, so you and Karen split, but that doesn't mean you have to spend the rest of your life alone. It takes two to make a marriage work, you know, and I warned you at the beginning that Karen wasn't the right woman for you."

Head down, hands in his pockets, Duke began prowling the room. "So you did, but it was mostly my fault that the marriage failed."

"Because you didn't have enough time for her?"

"Partly," Duke muttered, wondering what he had ever seen in Karen. Compared to Marnie, she was a shallow paper doll of a woman. But then no woman would ever compare favorably to Marnie.

"Man, you gave Karen every minute you could spare. I wish I'd been around to help relieve the pressure."

"You have your own company to worry about."

"Well, now that you're president, you can run this company the way you want. You can delegate more, can even take a holiday."

"Yeah, finally I'm free." Duke came to an abrupt halt in front of the company flag, laughed harshly, then swung and began pacing again, this time staying well clear of the flag.

"So, why don't you marry Marnie?" Dare's question was met with stony silence, and after waiting a moment, he continued, "Sorry, maybe I'm out of line. Maybe I read more into the situation than was there. I thought you loved her."

Duke stopped pacing and stood, staring at the family coat of arms that was hanging on the wall. "I do," he admitted softly, the words echoing in the empty, aching chambers of his heart.

"Then why don't you marry her?" Dare asked, his voice just as soft.

"Because I can't make her happy." Moving over to the desk, Duke sank into his chair and picked up a letter from the in-basket. "And that's all I'm going to say on the subject."

In one lithe movement Dare was on his feet and leaning over the desk. "Dammit, man, I'm your brother. Why won't you level with me?"

Duke gazed blankly at the letter as the ramifications of Dare's question sank in. Why hadn't he leveled with Marnie? Why hadn't he told her the truth the first night they had talked? Why had he let his infernal pride stand in the way of doing the honorable thing? Sure, he had walked away from her so she could get on with her life, but not until after he had hurt her. For that, he'd burn in hell.

"Duke, are you okay?"

Taking a deep breath, Duke raised his head and stared stonily at his brother. "No, not really, but I'll survive."

Dare stared back, waiting, and when Duke remained silent, he slapped the desk with the palm of his large hand. "I thought Dev and the Baron were the bullheaded men in this family, but I swear you could give them lessons." He banged the desk again, then turned and headed for the door.

"Where are you going?" Duke asked, half rising to his feet.

"I feel like kicking butt, so I'll go yell at my suppliers."

"Thanks, Dare."

Dare paused and glanced over his shoulder. "For what?"

"For being you. For caring."

"Well, if you decide you want to talk, I'll be

down the hall," Dare said, and giving a salute, left the room.

Duke sank back into the chair and looked around his office. Finally, he had gotten what he wanted; the company was his. But in reality he had nothing. The family coat of arms hanging on the wall and the company flag standing by the door mocked him more than ever. For his father was right; he was a failure. With a groan he dropped his head into his hands.

Giving the beaming secretary and the six Japanese businessmen in the outer office her best smile, Marnie silently opened the door to Duke's office, stepped inside, and just as silently closed the door behind her. She stood for a moment taking in the man who was sitting at the desk, his head bowed. When he didn't look up, she took another moment to glance around the office, noting the flag and the family coat of arms—symbols of a man who was proud of his heritage. Symbols Duke had once told her he wanted to pass on to his son.

Marnie patted the coral silk dress that covered her still-flat tummy, elated but slightly apprehensive about the fact that she carried his son, or maybe his daughter. Surely, Duke would be as proud as she was about the baby. Surely, Duke loved her. Hadn't he risked his life for her?

But if he did love her, why hadn't he come back

to her? she wondered, her gaze seeking the man who was still slumped over the desk. Duke was exhausted, she realized, her heart going out to him.

"Duke," she whispered in concern. "Are you all right?"

Duke's head flew up, and he shoved himself to his feet, staring in hungry disbelief at the beautiful redheaded woman before him. "Marnie, is it really you? I'm not dreaming, am I?"

"I—If you are, th-then I'm in it," she said, her voice breaking.

He rounded the desk, arms open, and she ran toward him, meeting him in the middle of the room. Flinging her arms around his neck, she pulled down his head to meet her eager lips.

He kissed her desperately, as though he were drowning and needed her for air. As though his heart had stopped beating, and he needed her to go on living. And it was true, Duke realized as he kissed her again. Loving Marnie had given him life, and life without Marnie wasn't worth living.

Eventually, he raised his head and gazed down at her, his chest heaving, his limbs trembling. She clung to him, staring back, her lips swollen with his kisses, her eyes luminous with love.

"Oh, Marnie, Marnie," he said, his voice choked with emotion. "You don't know how many times I've looked up and seen you standing in the doorway. And how many times I've woken in the night and felt you lying beside me."

"My bed has been so empty without you," she whispered. "So is my home . . . and my heart."

This time when he kissed her, his lips were softer, gentler, but no less demanding, and Marnie returned his kisses, giving him everything within her—all her love, her happiness, her bright, optimistic hope of a future together. Because although Duke didn't know it yet, they already had a joint stake in the future. And hopefully in many generations to come.

He didn't know what the future held, Duke thought with the one part of his brain that wasn't swamped by Marnie's kisses, but somehow Marnie had to be a part of it. Somehow, he had to find a way to make her dreams come true. Finally, reluctantly, he raised his head, but he continued to clasp her to him.

Marnie hugged Duke, listening to his pounding heart, waiting for him to tell her he loved her. Surely, he must love her, Marnie reassured herself. Otherwise he wouldn't keep kissing her, holding her. Surely, everything would work out all right.

"I kept wondering if my days with you had been a dream," he murmured as he dropped a kiss into her hair.

"It wasn't a dream, Duke. It was very real." She raised her head and smiled at him, her eyes brimming with happy tears. "And so is the baby I'm carrying inside me."

Duke drew back, staring at her in shocked dismay. "Baby?"

"Yes. Our baby." Marnie captured one of his hands and squeezed it between both of hers. "I'm sorry, I didn't mean to blurt it out like that, but I haven't told anyone else, and it is all so new and exciting that I was bursting to tell you."

"Marnie . . ."

"I know this is a surprise to you. I know I told you that I was protected, but you see I had forgotten to take the pills along with me. So I guess we're having a baby."

"Marnie . . ." He swallowed hard and somehow managed to pull his hand away from hers. "The baby isn't mine."

Her hands flew to her stomach, protecting her child as she stared at him in confusion. "Not yours?"

"No, it can't be."

"Why not?" she asked, wondering why something that should be so joyous was turning into a nightmare. Why would Duke question, even for one second, that he was the father?

"Because I can't have children."

Shocked, she sank onto a chair and pressed her shaking knees together. "There m-must be some m-mistake," she stammered.

"Yeah, I guess you could say that," Duke whispered, his throat so tight, he could barely speak.

"Why . . ." She drew in a shaky breath and

tried again. "Why do you think you can't have children?"

He backed up against the desk, sat down on the corner, and gripped the edges with white-knuckled hands. Fate, it seemed, had a sneaky way of testing a man, tempting him with a glimpse of heaven when giving in to temptation would mean hell. Lord, how he loved Marnie. Loved her so much, he would even marry her and give her child his name. But he could never claim it as his, because Marnie would eventually learn the truth. The truth he should have told her months ago.

Taking a deep breath, he spoke the words he knew would shatter any hope that he could ever marry Marnie. "Because Karen and I tried for years to have a child, and we couldn't. Remember, I told you?"

"Well, it must have been Karen who was infertile," she said, gazing at him, her eyes full of conviction.

The belief in her eyes was almost his undoing, but he forced himself to keep looking at her. "No, it wasn't," he said huskily. "I gave her the divorce because she was pregnant with John's baby."

"She had a child?"

"Yeah, which makes it very obvious why *we* couldn't have any."

"There still must be some mistake," said Marnie, frowning at him in puzzlement. It was all so confusing, she could barely take it in, and the fear that her hopes and dreams were going to go down with the *Titanic*, after all, made it difficult to think.

"I'm sorry, Marnie, that I didn't level with you the night we played poker and you told me how much you wanted children. I should have told you then that I couldn't have any. I should have ended things between us before they started." He rocked back and forth slightly, as if in pain. "But I was selfish, Marnie, and less than honorable, and for that I'm deeply sorry."

Silently, she digested his words, her eyes never leaving his. "But you still don't believe the baby I'm carrying is yours?" she asked slowly, beginning to sort things out in her mind.

"Nooo," he said, the word sounding like a moan.

"So you think I'm trying to palm someone else's child off on you?"

He murmured something she couldn't hear, and she rose to stand proudly before him, fighting to control the tears of anger, frustration, and hurt that threatened to fall.

"Fine, Duke, go on believing Karen, the woman who cheated on you," she cried out in anguish. "For heaven's sake, don't believe in me. After all, I'm only the woman who loves you."

"Marnie . . ."

He pushed himself upright and stared down at her, his eyes as somber as a rainy day. She backed away from him, her hands raised to ward him off.

"I'm sorry, Duke. I thought I could help you, could heal your hurt." She laughed softly, sadly. "But no matter how hard I tried, I couldn't pull off that miracle. Because I can't help a man who doesn't have a believing heart." She continued to back toward the door.

He followed, his hand outstretched. "Marnie, at least let me—"

"No, Duke, I don't want anything from you," she said, her hand groping to find the knob. "Not now, or when your child is born. We'll manage fine on our own."

Opening the door, she stepped into the outer office and smiled weakly at the six men who were still waiting there. "Thank you for your patience, gentlemen, he's all yours."

She bolted down the hall, ignoring the uproar she'd left behind and the way Duke called out her name. Rounding the corner, she ran full tilt into a tall, solid man, who grunted as he grabbed her.

"Marnie!"

"Dare!" she whispered, clutching him as though he were a safety net.

"You've come to see Duke?"

"I've seen him, and now I want out of here."

Dare took one look at the tears that were brimming in her eyes, then hustled her out of the building and into his Ford pickup, all the while calling his brother every low-down name he could think of in five different languages.

Once in the truck, Marnie began to cry in earnest, and Dare drove through the streets of Houston one-handed, while he patted her shoulder and handed her tissues with the other. Finally, she stopped crying, blew her nose, and gave him a watery smile.

"Sorry. I seem to be crying a lot these days."

"Y'all care to tell me what's wrong?" Dare drawled softly.

Marnie sighed. "It's Duke."

"Don't tell me the fool is still refusing to admit you're the best thing that's ever happened to him?"

"Worse than that, he doesn't believe in me." Marnie sniffed and dabbed at her eyes, feeling as if her world had come to an end. "I told him once that I never lie, but he chooses to believe Karen rather than me."

"Lie about what?"

"Our baby."

"You're pregnant?" Dare smiled at Marnie in delight.

"Yes, and Duke doesn't believe the baby is his," Marnie said, too distraught by Duke's unexpected reaction to her news to be embarrassed because she had blurted it out to his brother. "He thinks he can't have children. Can you imagine that!"

Dare thumped the steering wheel with a clenched fist. "Oh, Lord, so that's what's been bugging him all these years. If only I had known."

"Why would he believe he can't have children?"

"Because he's been told a pack of lies since the day he met Karen."

Dare's words barely registered, and Marnie continued to speak. "I thought that when Duke learned I was pregnant, a miracle would happen, and he would want to marry me, but I was wrong. He doesn't even love me."

"Oh yes, he does, Marnie."

Sadly, she shook her head. "He's never once told me he loves me."

"Give him a chance to get over the shock," Dare reached out to squeeze her hand. "I'm sure he'll come to his senses."

Maybe Duke did love her, Marnie thought, allowing herself a brief ray of hope. Maybe his mistaken belief that he couldn't give her a child had kept him from declaring his love.

"Well, I'm not about to wait around," she said, suddenly feeling too exhausted and heartsore to let the hope burn any brighter. "Would you take me to the airport?"

"I'd rather take you out to the ranch and let Madre look after you."

"No, I want to go home." Marnie managed a wan smile. "Your mother will be welcome to see the baby after the birth, but right now I want to go home."

"You're right. Home is the best place for you." Releasing her hand, Dare reached for the cellular phone. "I'll ask the pilot to get the company jet ready."

A half hour later Dare was helping her into the jet. "I'd like to come along, Marnie," he said as he settled her into the plush seat and fastened her seat belt. "But I've got to leave for Kuwait tomorrow, and I need to tell my brother a few facts of life before I go. Facts I should have told him a long time ago." He touched her hair, then brushed a kiss against her temple. "Don't give up on him, Marnie. Duke needs someone like you. Someone who believes in him."

Duke was prowling his empty office as if he were a wounded mountain lion when Dare entered with a legal file folder in his hand.

"Well, Duke, you'll be happy to know that Marnie is winging her way out of your life," he said as he dropped into his normal reclining position in the big chair.

Duke stopped pacing and stared at him. "You saw her? She was with you?"

"Yeah."

"Thank God. No one seemed to know what happened to her. How did she look?"

"Outside of the fact that she cried all the way to the airport, she looked like a proud mother-to-be."

"She told you about the baby?" Duke asked, collapsing into his chair because he suddenly didn't have the strength to stand.

Dare sat up, leaned forward, and fixed Duke with a disapproving eye. "Yeah, and I'm debating what to do first. Thrash you within an inch of your life for getting her into trouble, or kick you into the next state for telling her the baby isn't yours."

"She told you I can't have children?"

"She told me you *think* you can't have children. She happens to believe you can. So tell me, Big Brother, now that you've had a chance to get over the shock, what do you really believe?"

"That Marnie is having my baby," Duke said quietly, but with total certainty.

Dare let out an audible sigh. "Why are you so certain?"

"Because Marnie never lies. It's as simple as that." Duke passed a weary hand over his face. "Which means that Karen lied to me." He paused, still trying to take it all in, still trying to make sense out of what had happened four years ago. "When Karen asked for a divorce, I refused, but when she told me she wanted to marry John because he had given her the one thing she wanted, the one thing I couldn't give her . . . a child . . . I agreed."

"Why didn't you tell any of us what was happening? We wanted to help you, but you shut us out."

"Because I was devastated," Duke admitted. "And too proud to let any of you know how badly I hurt."

Dare nodded, his brown eyes full of compassion. "So you gave me all the genealogical information you had dug up to pass on to my son."

"Yeah."

"I thank you for the sentiment, but I sure as hell wish you'd told me why you were giving it to me. Maybe I could have saved you a lot of heartache."

Silence reigned for a few minutes while Dare stared at the file in his hand, and Duke gazed blindly at the top of his desk. Finally, Duke raised his head and looked at Dare.

"Why would Karen have done such a thing?" Duke asked, still trying to come to grips with the shambles Karen had made of his life. All along he had accepted the blame for everything, and it was still difficult to believe that Karen would have deliberately lied to him. "Why would she have told me it was my fault we couldn't have children?"

"To get you to give her a divorce so she could marry John." Dare tapped the edge of the folder against his knee. "She'd wanted him for years, you know, probably since the day he showed up at the ranch shortly after y'all were married. Although he was crazy about her, he wouldn't have anything to do with her because he was your friend. Then she figured out his weakness. He desperately wanted a child to inherit his fortune. So had you, of course, and she had known that and had played on it to get you to marry her. Then she made damn good and sure that y'all didn't have a child." He rolled the folder into a cylinder. "It would have ruined her figure, spoiled her dinner parties, interfered with her fun. No, she didn't want a child, but when she realized it was the only way she could trap John, she baited the hook, and he took it."

As Duke listened to his brother's words, he realized how blind he'd been about Karen and their marriage. "How the hell did you figure out all that?" he asked, shaking his head in amazement.

"I have eyes, and I do my thinking with my brain, not my—" He pointed the rolled file at Duke. "For a smart businessman you were completely blind when it came to Karen, but you weren't the only man she fooled. She wanted you because you were rich and handsome. John isn't quite as handsome, but he's a hell of a lot richer, and better still, he doesn't have to work for his money, so he has plenty of time to be at her beck and call. Karen wanted him. Now that she's got him, she's casting her eye on the governor."

"Dare, you are one discerning son of a gun."

"No, Duke, if I were such a hotshot, I would've brought this to you years ago, but I didn't want to hurt you." He began unrolling the folder, and tried to flatten it out against his knee.

"What is it?"

"Records from an investigator I hired to trail Karen, just in case she ever wanted a divorce. When I learned she wasn't taking you to the cleaner's, I decided this was one gift I wasn't going to give to you." He laid the report down in front of Duke. "I give it to you now."

"What's in it?" Duke asked, almost afraid to open the folder.

"Medical records from a little hospital out of state," Dare said, then watched in silence as Duke slowly opened the folder and read the report.

Duke raised his head and stared at Dare, his eyes bright with tears. "Karen had an abortion?"

"Yeah."

Duke swallowed hard. "She killed my baby."

Dare nodded, then sat helplessly as Duke bowed his head and wept.

Marnie wept as the plane winged its way west with the setting sun. And she wept the next day when a King Oil helicopter delivered a package to her from Dare, containing all the genealogical information Duke had collected.

This is for your son, Dare had written. *And please don't give up on his father. Remember, Duke needs someone to believe in him.*

"Well," Marnie told her little one as she dried her tears, "We *do* believe in your daddy, don't we? And we're certainly not going to give up on him. Let's pretend we are living in old Colonial Victoria and are waiting for him to come home from sea. He's on a trading trip to China, and when he comes home, he'll bring us the greatest treasure of all, his love."

Marnie waited the next day and the next, and continued to pretend, knowing full well that if Duke didn't come soon, she would have to tell her parents about her baby and begin making plans. But meanwhile she would wait and pretend and dream.

He came to her in her dreams on the seventh night, dressed as a pirate, and the next morning when she looked up from her workbench and saw the tall ship sail into the harbor, she thought she was still dreaming.

But the ship was real, she realized as she heard the orders being barked, saw the sails come down, and saw her father leave the shed on the run to help tie the *Silver Cloud* to the dock.

Marnie followed him out and stood by, watching as a tall man dressed in black walked toward the flagpole and ran down the flag—the black, green, and gold flag. Then, walking the gangplank, he came directly to her and bowed low before her.

"I have come, fair Venus, to beg you to grant me three wishes," Duke said softly, his head still bowed.

"Oh, Duke," she whispered, "please look at me."

Slowly, he raised his head and looked at her, and she gasped when she saw the glimmer of tears in his eyes.

"Would you please accept this flag, Marnie, and keep it safe to give to my son?" he asked, holding out the flag to her.

She took it and clutched it to her breast. "I'll keep it safe, always, as I will keep him safe," she vowed.

Gently releasing one of her hands from the flag,

he raised it to his lips. "Along with the flag, will you please accept my heart?"

"Is yours a believing heart?" she asked, barely able to say the words.

"Yes," he said huskily. "My heart believes in you, and it believes in me."

"Then I accept it. Gladly."

"Now for my final request." Slowly, elegantly, he went down on bended knee. "Will you marry me, Marnie?"

Her heart ached to say yes, but her head wouldn't let her. "I don't know," she said.

He continued to gaze up at her, his eyes alight with silver. "You once told me you'd never marry a man who needed you, but I need you, Marnie, to fill my days with laughter and my nights with loving." He bowed his head, resting it against her tummy. "I need you, Marnie, to be the mother of my children, and to be beside me when I'm old and gray. I need you to bring old boats and orphans and forgotten people into my life. In short, I need you, Marnie, to make my life complete." He raised his head and looked at her again, his eyes shining with hope. "But I also love you, Marnie, and I will love you for the rest of my days and beyond. I fell in love with you in the Land West of the Sun and East of the Moon, but I love you here and now, and wherever you will take me in the future. I love you so much, Marnie, that I would lay down my life for you. Will you marry me?"

Suddenly, Marnie was laughing and crying and

saying, "Yes! Yes! Yes, David. I'll marry you," and raining kisses as well as tears on Duke's upturned face.

And the deckhands began cheering and blowing whistles, and the boatyard crew began clapping, and Bill MacBride began making noises in his throat, while Moyra MacBride, who had joined her husband, blew her nose and wiped her eyes.

Duke rose to his feet and stood with his arm around Marnie as she introduced him to her parents. After explanations, then more tears and hugs and kisses of congratulations, Duke led his new family up the gangplank and onto the deck of the tall ship. A grinning bos'n began pipping the whistle, then the first mate stepped forward and gave Duke a roll of parchment.

Duke turned to Marnie, saluted her, then handed her the parchment. "Your ship, Captain," he said, saluting her again.

Giving him a puzzled look, Marnie unrolled the paper and read the words. "You bought this ship?" she asked breathlessly, raising wide eyes to search his face. "For me?"

Duke half smiled, thinking that the pleased look on Marnie's face made the long week of intense negotiations to buy the brigantine worthwhile. He could only hope that Marnie would also forgive him for waiting until he had the ship before he came to her. "You wanted her for your program, and I figured I could use her as a bribe if you were reluctant to marry me."

"Oh, Duke. I've never wanted anything from you except your love."

Duke smiled then, finally believing that everything would be all right. "You have all of my love, Marnie, always and into the hereafter."

"And I'll love you forever too," she vowed, reaching up to give him a kiss. It was many minutes before she glanced at the parchment again. She read further, then looked up at Duke, her eyes full of tears. "Duke! You've renamed the ship."

He nodded, smiling down at her, his eyes full of love. "From now on, she'll be called the *Believing Heart.*"

But it wasn't until that night, when they were lying together on her seashell bed, that Duke told her the horrible cost he had paid for his believing heart. And because his wound was still raw and bleeding, his tears seeped onto her breast.

"Oh, Duke, my love, let me love you," Marnie said. "Let me take away your pain." And because she was Marnie, the mender of broken boats and houses, the healer of hurt animals, the friend of forgotten people, she worked her loving magic upon him . . . and took the pain from his eyes, his heart, and his soul.

THE EDITOR'S CORNER

The heroines in September's LOVESWEPT novels have a secret dream of love and passion—and they find the answer to their wishes with FANTASY MEN! Whether he's a dangerous rogue, a dashing prince, or a lord of the jungle, he's a masterful hero who knows just the right moves that dazzle the senses, the teasing words that stoke white-hot desire, and the seductive caresses that promise ecstasy. He's the kind of man who can make a woman do anything, the only man who can fulfill her deepest longing. And the heroines find they'll risk all, even their hearts, to make their dreams come true with FANTASY MEN. . . .

Our first dream lover sizzles off the pages of Sandra Chastain's **THE MORNING AFTER**, LOVESWEPT #636. Razor Cody had come to Savannah seeking revenge on the man who'd destroyed his business, but instead he found a fairy-tale princess whose violet eyes and spun-gold hair made him yearn for what he'd never dared to hope would be his! Rachel Kimble told him she'd known he was coming and hinted of the treasure he'd find if he stayed, but she couldn't conceal her shocking desire for the mysterious stranger! Vowing to keep her safe from shadows that haunted her nights, Razor fought to heal Rachel's pain, as her gentle touch soothed his own. **THE MORNING AFTER** is Sandra Chastain at her finest.

Cindy Gerard invites you to take one last summer swim with her fantasy man in **DREAM TIDE, LOVESWEPT #637**. Patrick Ryan was heart-stoppingly gorgeous—all temptation and trouble in a pair of jeans. And Merry Clare Thomas was stunned to wake up in his arms . . . and in his bed! She'd taken refuge in her rental cottage, never expecting the tenant to return that night—or that he'd look exactly like the handsome wanderer of a hundred years ago who'd been making steamy love to her in her dreams every night for a week. Was it destiny or just coincidence that Pat called her his flame, his firebrand, just as her dream lover had? Overwhelmed by need, dazzled by passion, Merry responded with fierce pleasure to Pat's wildfire caresses, possessed by him in a magical enchantment that just couldn't be real. But Cindy's special touch is all too real in this tale of a fantasy come true.

TROUBLE IN PARADISE, LOVESWEPT #638, is another winner from one of LOVESWEPT's rising stars, Susan Connell. Just lying in a hammock, Reilly Anderson awakened desire potent enough to take her breath away, but Allison Richards fought her attraction to the bare-chested hunk who looked like he'd stepped out of an adventure movie! Gazing at the long-legged vision who insisted that he help her locate her missing brother-in-law, Reilly knew that trouble had arrived . . . the kind of trouble a man just had to taste! Reilly drew her into a paradise of pleasure, freeing her spirit with tender savagery and becoming her very own Tarzan, Lord of the Jungle. He swore he'd make her see she had filled his heart with joy and that he'd never let her go.

Linda Jenkins's fantasy is a **SECRET ADMIRER**, LOVESWEPT #639. An irresistible rascal, Jack was the golden prince of her secret girlhood fantasies, but Kary Lucas knew Jack Rowland could never be hers! Back then he'd always teased her about being the smartest girl in town—how could she believe the charming nomad with the bad-boy grin when he insisted he was home to stay at last? Jack infuriated her and made her ache with sensual longing. But when mysterious gifts began arriving, presents and notes that seemed to know her private passions, Kary was torn: tempted by the romance of her unknown knight, yet thrilled by the explosive heat of Jack's embraces, the insatiable need he aroused. Linda's fantasy man has just the right combination of dreamy mystery and thrilling reality to keep your nights on fire!

Terry Lawrence works her own unique LOVESWEPT magic with **DANCING ON THE EDGE,** LOVE-SWEPT #640. Stunt coordinator Greg Ford needed a woman to stand up to him, to shake him up, and Annie Oakley Cartwright decided she was just the brazen daredevil to do it! Something burned between them from the moment they met, made Annie want to rise to his challenge, to tempt the man who made her lips tingle just by looking. Annie trusted him with her body, ached to ease his sorrow with her rebel's heart. Once she'd reminded him life was a series of gambles, and love the biggest one of all, she could only hope he would dance with his spitfire as long as their music played. Terry's spectacular romance will send you looking for your own stuntman!

Leanne Banks has a regal fantasy man for you in **HIS ROYAL PLEASURE**, LOVESWEPT #641. Prince Alex swept into her peaceful life like a swashbuckling pirate, confidently expecting Katherine Kendall to let him spend a month at her island camp—never confessing the secret of his birth to the sweet and tender lady who made him want to break all the rules! He made her feel beautiful, made her dream of dancing in the dark and succumbing to forbidden kisses under a moonlit sky. Katherine wondered who he was, but Alex was an expert when it came to games lovers play, and he made her moan with ecstasy at his sizzling touch . . . until she learned his shocking secret. Leanne is at her steamy best with this sexy fantasy man.

Happy reading!

With warmest wishes,

Nita Taublib

Associate Publisher

P.S. On the next pages is a preview of the Bantam titles on sale *now* at your favorite bookstore.

Don't miss these exciting books by your
favorite Bantam authors

On sale in July:
FANTA C
by Sandra Brown

CRY WOLF
by Tami Hoag

TWICE IN A LIFETIME
by Christy Cohen

THE TESTIMONY
by Sharon and Tom Curtis

And in hardcover from Doubleday
STRANGER IN MY ARMS
by R. J. Kaiser

From *New York Times*
Bestselling Author

Sandra Brown

Fanta C

The bestselling author of Temperatures Rising *and*
French Silk, *Sandra Brown has created a sensation with her
contemporary novels. Now, in this classic novel she offers a
tender, funny, and deeply sensual story about a woman
caught between the needs of her children, her career, and her
own passionate heart.*

Elizabeth Burke's days are filled with the business of
running an elegant boutique and caring for her two
small children. But her nights are long and empty
since the death of her husband two years before,
and she spends them dreaming of the love and romance
that might have been. Then Thad Randolph steps
into her life—a man right out of her most intimate
fantasies.

Elizabeth doesn't believe in fairy tales, and she knows
all too well that happy endings happen only in books.
Now she wishes she could convince herself that friend-

ship is all she wants from Thad. But the day will come when she'll finally have to make a choice—to remain forever true to her memories or to let go of the past and risk loving once more.

Cry Wolf
by
Tami Hoag

author of *Still Waters* and *Lucky's Lady*

Tami Hoag is one of today's premier writers of romantic suspense. Publisher's Weekly calls her "a master of the genre" for her powerful combination of gripping suspense and sizzling passion. Now from the incredibly talented author of Sarah's Sin, Lucky's Lady, *and* Still Waters *comes* Cry Wolf, *her most dangerously thrilling novel yet. . . .*

All attorney Laurel Chandler wanted was a place to hide, to escape the painful memories of a case that had destroyed her career, her marriage, and nearly her life. But coming home to the peaceful, tree-lined streets of her old hometown won't give Laurel the serenity she craves. For in the sultry heat of a Louisiana summer, she'll find herself pursued by Jack Boudreaux, a gorgeous stranger whose carefree smile hides a private torment . . . and by a murderer who enjoys the hunt as much as the kill.

In the following scene, Laurel is outside of Frenchie's, a local hangout, when she realizes she's unable to drive the car she borrowed. When Jack offers to drive her home, she has no alternative but to accept.

"Women shouldn't accept rides from men they barely know," she said, easing herself down in the bucket seat, her gaze fixed on Jack.

"What?" he asked, splaying a hand across his bare chest, the picture of hurt innocence. "You think *I'm* the Bayou Strangler? Oh, man . . ."

"You could be the man."

"What makes you think it's a man? Could be a woman."

"Could be, but not likely. Serial killers tend to be white males in their thirties."

He grinned wickedly, eyes dancing. "Well, I fit that bill, I guess, but I don't have to kill ladies to get what I want, angel."

He leaned into her space, one hand sliding across the back of her seat, the other edging along the dash, corralling her. Laurel's heart kicked into overdrive as he came closer, though fear was not the dominant emotion. It should have been, but it wasn't.

That strange sense of desire and anticipation crept along her nerves. If she leaned forward, he would kiss her. She could see the promise in his eyes and felt something wild and reckless and completely foreign to her rise up in answer, pushing her to close the distance, to take the chance. His eyes dared her, his mouth lured—masculine, sexy, lips slightly parted in invitation. What fear she felt was of herself, of this attraction she didn't want.

"It's power, not passion," she whispered, barely able to find her voice at all.

Jack blinked. The spell was broken. "What?"

"They kill for power. Exerting power over other human beings gives them a sense of omnipotence . . . among other things."

He sat back and fired the 'Vette's engine, his brows drawn as he contemplated what she'd said. "So, why are you going with me?"

"Because there are a dozen witnesses standing on the gallery who saw me get in the car with you. You'd be the last person seen with me alive, which would automatically make you a suspect. Patrons in the bar will testify that I spurned your advances. That's motive. If you were the killer, you'd be pretty stupid to take me away from here and kill me, and if this killer was stupid, someone would have caught him by now."

He scowled as he put the car in gear. "And here I thought you'd say it was my charm and good looks."

"Charming men don't impress me," she said flatly, buckling her seat belt.

Then what does? Jack wondered as he guided the car slowly out of the parking lot. A sharp mind, a man of principles? He had one, but wasn't the other. Not that it mattered. He wasn't interested in Laurel Chandler. She would be too much trouble. And she was too uptight to go for a man who spent most of his waking hours at Frenchie's—unlike her sister, who went for any man who could get it up. Night and day, those two. He couldn't help wondering why.

The Chandler sisters had been raised to be belles. Too good for the likes of him, ol' Blackie would have said. Too good for a no-good coonass piece of trash. He glanced across at Laurel, who sat with her hands folded and her glasses perched on her slim little nose and thought the old man would have been right. She was prim and proper, Miss Law and Order, full of morals and high ideals and upstanding qualities . . . and fire . . . and pain . . . and secrets in her eyes. . . .

"Was I to gather from that conversation with T-Grace that you used to be an attorney?" she asked as they turned onto Dumas and headed back toward downtown.

He smiled, though it held no real amusement, only cynicism. "Sugar, 'attorney' is too polite a word for what I used to be. I was a corporate shark for Tristar Chemical."

Laurel tried to reconcile the traditional three-piece-suit corporate image with the man who sat across from her, a baseball cap jammed down backward on his head, his Hawaiian shirt hanging open to reveal the hard, tanned body of a light heavyweight boxer. "What happened?"

What happened? A simple question as loaded as a shotgun that had been primed and pumped. What happened? He had succeeded. He had set out to prove to his old man that he could do something, be something, make big money. It hadn't mattered that Blackie was long dead and gone to hell.

The old man's ghost had driven him. He had succeeded, and in the end he had lost everything.

"I turned on 'em," he said, skipping the heart of the story. The pain he endured still on Evie's behalf was his own private hell. He didn't share it with anyone. "*Rogue Lawyer*. I think they're gonna make it into a TV movie one of these days."

"What do you mean, you turned on them?"

"I mean, I unraveled the knots I'd tied for them in the paper trail that divorced them from the highly illegal activities of shipping and dumping hazardous waste," he explained, not entirely sure why he was telling her. Most of the time when people asked, he just blew it off, made a joke, and changed the subject. "The Feds took a dim view of the company. The company gave me the ax, and the Bar Association kicked my ass out."

"You were disbarred for revealing illegal, potentially dangerous activities to the federal government?" Laurel said, incredulous. "But that's—"

"The way it is, sweetheart," he growled, slowing the 'Vette as the one and only stop light in Bayou Breaux turned red. He rested his hand on the stick shift and gave Laurel a hard look. "Don' make me out to be a hero, sugar. I'm nobody's saint. I lost it," he said bitterly. "I crashed and burned. I went down in a ball of flame, and I took the company with me. I had my reasons, and none of them had anything to do with such noble causes as the protection of the environment."

"But—"

"'But,' you're thinking now, 'mebbe this Jack, he isn't such a bad guy after all,' yes?" His look turned sly, speculative. He chuckled as she frowned. She didn't want to think he could read her so easily. If they'd been playing poker, he would have cleaned out her pockets.

"Well, you're wrong, angel," he murmured darkly, his mouth twisting with bitter amusement as her blue eyes widened. "I'm as bad as they come." Then he flashed his famous grin, dimples biting into his cheeks. "But I'm a helluva good time."

Twice in a Lifetime
by
Christy Cohen

author of *Private Scandals*

Fifteen years ago, an act of betrayal tore four best friends apart . . .

SARAH. *A lonely newlywed in a new town, she was thrilled when Annabel came into her life. Suddenly Sarah had someone to talk to and the best part was that her husband seemed to like Annabel too.*

JESSE. *With his sexy good looks and dangerous aura, he could have had any woman. But he'd chosen sweet, innocent Sarah, who touched not only his body but his soul. So why couldn't Jesse stop dreaming of his wife's best friend?*

ANNABEL. *Beautiful, desirable, and enigmatic, she yearned for something more exciting than being a wife and mother. And nothing was more exciting than making a man like Jesse want her.*

PATRICK. *Strong and tender, this brilliant scientist learned that the only way to keep Annabel his wife was to turn a blind eye—until the day came when he couldn't pretend anymore.*

In the following scene, Jesse and Annabel feel trapped at a birthday party that Sarah is hosting and they have to escape into the surrounding neighborhood.

As they walked through the neighborhood of newer homes, Jesse's arm was around her. He could feel every curve of her. Her breast was pressed against his chest. Her leg brushed his as she walked.

"Sarah's probably pissed," he said.

Annabel laughed. "She'll get over it. Besides, Patrick the knight will save her."

Jesse looked at her.

"Have you noticed they've been talking to each other a lot?"

"Of course. Patrick calls her from work. And sometimes at night. He's too honest not to tell me."

When Annabel pressed herself closer to Jesse, he lowered his hand a little on her shoulder. An inch or two farther down and he would be able to touch the silky skin of her breast.

"Do you love him?" he asked.

Annabel stopped suddenly and Jesse dropped his hand. She turned to stare at him.

"What do you think?"

With her eyes challenging him, Jesse took a step closer.

"I think you don't give a fuck about him. Maybe you did when you married him, but it didn't last long. Now it's me you're after."

Annabel tossed back her black hair, laughing.

"God, what an ego. You think a little harmless flirting means I'm hot for you. No wonder Sarah needed a change of pace."

Jesse grabbed her face in one hand and squeezed. He watched tears come to her eyes as he increased the pressure on her jaw, but she didn't cry out.

"Sarah did not cheat on me," he said. "You got the story wrong."

He pushed her away and started walking back toward the house. Annabel took a deep breath, then came after him.

"What Sarah did or didn't do isn't the point," she said when she reached him. "She's not the one who's unhappy."

Jesse glanced at her, but kept walking.

"You're saying I am?"

"It's obvious, Jesse. Little Miss Perfect Sarah isn't all that exciting. Especially for a man like you. I'll bet that's why you have to ride your Harley all the time. To replace all the passion you gave up when you married her."

Jesse looked up over the houses, to Mt. Rainier in the distance.

"I sold the bike," he said. "Two weeks ago."

"My God, why?"

Jesse stopped again.

"Because Sarah asked me to. And because, no matter what you think, I love her."

They stared at each other for a long time. The wind was cool and Jesse watched gooseflesh prickle Annabel's skin. He didn't know whom he was trying to convince more, Annabel or himself.

"I think we should go back," Jesse said.

Annabel nodded. "Of course. You certainly don't want to make little Sarah mad. You've got to be the dutiful husband. If Sarah says sell your bike, you sell your bike. If she wants you to entertain twelve kids like a clown, then you do it. If—"

Jesse grabbed her, only intending to shut her up. But when he looked down at her, he knew she had won. She had been whittling away at him from the very beginning. She had made him doubt himself, and Sarah, and everything he thought he should be. He grabbed her hair and tilted her head back. She slid her hands up around his neck. Her fingers were cool and silky.

Later, he would look back and try to convince himself that she was the one who initiated the kiss, that she pulled his head down and pressed her red lips to his. Maybe she initiated it, maybe he did. All he knew was that he was finally touching her, kissing her, his tongue was in her mouth and it felt better than he'd ever imagined.

The Testimony

A classic romance by

Sharon & Tom Curtis

bestselling authors of *The Golden Touch*

It had been so easy falling in love with Jesse Ludan . . . with his ready smile and laughing green eyes, his sensual body and clever journalist's mind. The day Christine became his wife was the happiest day of her life. But for the past six months, Jesse's idealism has kept him in prison. And now he's coming home a hero . . . and a stranger.

In the following scene Jesse and Christine are alone in the toolshed behind her house only hours after Jesse's return . . .

"Jess?" Her blue eyes had grown solemn.

"What, love?"

"I don't know how to ask this . . . Jesse, I don't want to blast things out of you that you're not ready to talk about but I have to know . . ." An uncertain pause. "How much haven't you told me? Was prison . . . was it horrible?"

Was it horrible? she had asked him. There she stood in her silk knit sweater, her Gucci shoes, and one of the expensive skirts she wore that clung, but never too tightly, to her slender thighs, asking him if prison was horrible. Her eyes were serious and bright with the fetching sincerity that seemed like such a poor defense against the darker aspects of life and that, paradoxically, always made him want to bare his soul to that uncallused sanity. The soft taut skin over her nose and cheeks shone slightly in the highly filtered light, paling her freckles, giving a fragility to her face with its combined suggestion of sturdiness and sensitivity. He would have thought four years of marriage might have banished any unease he felt about what a sociologist would label the "class difference" of their backgrounds, yet looking at her now, he had never felt it more strongly.

There was a reel of fishing line in his right hand. Where had it come from? The window shelf. He let her thick curl slide from his fingers and walked slowly to the shelf, reaching up to replace the roll, letting the motion hide his face while he spoke.

"It was a little horrible." He leaned his back against the workbench, gripping the edge. Gently shifting the focus away from himself, he said, "Was it a little horrible here without me?"

"It was a lot horrible here without you." The admission seemed to relieve some of her tension. "Not that I'm proud of being so dependent on a man, mind you."

"Say three Our Fathers, two Hail Marys, and read six months of back issues of *Ms.* magazine. Go in peace, Daughter, and sin no more." He gestured a blessing. Then, putting a palm lightly over his own heart, he added, "I had the same thing. Desolation."

"You missed the daily dose of me?"

"I missed the daily dose of you."

Her toes turned inward, freckled fingers threaded anxiously together. The round chin dropped and she gazed at him from under her lashes, a mime of bashfulness.

"So here we are—alone at last," she breathed.

Sometimes mime was a game for Christine, sometimes a refuge. In college she had joined a small troupe that passed a hat in the city parks. To combat her shyness, she still used it, retreating as though to the anonymity of whiteface and costume.

He could feel the anxiety pent up in her. *Show me you're all right, Jesse.* Something elemental in his life seemed to hinge on his comforting her. He searched desperately for the self he had been before prison, trying to clone the person she would know and recognize and feel safe with.

"Alone, and in such romantic surroundings," he said, taking a step toward her. His heel touched a shovel blade, sending a shiver of reaction through the nervously perched lawn implements that lined the wall. Some interesting quirk of physics kept them upright except for one rake that came whacking to the floor at his feet. "Ah, the hazards of these secret liaisons! We've got to stop meeting like this—the gardener is beginning to suspect."

"The gardener I can handle, but when a man in his prime is nearly cut down by a rake . . ."

"A *dangerous* rake." His voice lowered. "This, my dear, is Milwaukee's most notorious rake. More women have surrendered their virtue to him than to the legions of Caesar." He lifted the rake tines upward and made it walk toward her, giving it a lascivious whisper. "Don't fight it, *cara*. Your body was made for love. With me you can experience the fullness of your womanhood."

She laughed at his notion of the things rakes say, garnered three years ago from a teasing thumb-through of a certain deliciously fat romance novel that she had meant to keep better hidden. Raising one hand dramatically to ward off the rake, she said, "Leaf me alone, lecher!"

The rake took an offended dip and marched back to the wall in a huff. "Reject me if you must," it said in a wounded tone, "but must I endure a bad pun about my honorable profession? I thought women were supposed to love a rake," it added hopefully.

A smile hovered near the edge of her husband's mobile lips. Christine recognized a certain quality in it that made her heart beat harder. As his hands came lightly down on her shoulders, her lips parted without her will and her gaze traveled up to meet the shadow play of desire in his eyes.

"Some women prefer their very own husbands." There was a slight breathless quiver in her voice, and the throb of tightening pressure in her lungs.

"Hot damn. A compliment." Jesse let his thumbs slide down the front of her shoulders, rotating them with gentle sensuality over the soft flesh that lay above the rise of her breasts. She had begun to tremble under the sure movements of his fingers, and her slipping control brought back to him all the warm nights they had shared, the tangled sheets, the pungent musky air. He remembered the rosy flush of her upraised nipples and the way they felt on his lips. . . .

It had been so long, more than six months, since they had been together, six months since he had even seen a woman. He wondered if she realized that, or guessed how her nearness made his senses skyrocket. He wanted her to give up her body to him, to offer herself to him like an expanding breath for him to touch and taste and fill, to watch her bluebell eyes grow smoky with rapture. But though he drew her close so that he could feel the lovely fullness of her small breasts pressing into his ribs, he made no move to lower his hands or to take her lips. She seemed entrancingly clean, like a just-bathed child, and as pure. The damaged part of him came to her almost as a supplicant, unwhole before her wholesomeness. Can I touch you, love? Tell me it's all right . . .

She couldn't have heard his thoughts, or seen them, because he had learned too well to disguise them; yet her hands came to him like an answer, her fingers entwined behind his neck, pulling him toward her warm mouth. He took a breath as her lips skimmed over his and another much harder one as she stood on her toes to heighten the contact. Her tongue probed shyly at his lips and then forced an entrance, her body twisting slowly into his, a sinuous shock against his thighs.

He murmured something, random words of desire he couldn't remember as he said them; the pressure of her lips increased, and he felt thought begin to leave, and a growing pressure behind his eyelids. His hands were drifting over her blindly, as in a vision, until a shuddering fever ran through his veins and he dragged her close, pulling her hard into him, holding her there with one arm while the other slid under her sweater, his fingers spreading over the powdery softness of her skin. A surprised moan swept from her mouth into his lips as his hand lightly covered her breast. His palm absorbed her warmth, her delicate shape, and the thrillingly uneven pattern of her respiration before slipping to the fine heat and velvet distension of her nipple.

This time he heard his own whisper, telling her that he loved her, that she bewitched him, and then repeating her name again and again with the rhythm of his mouth and tongue. He was overcome, lost in her elemental femaleness, his pulse hammering through his body. Leaning her back, bringing his mouth hard against hers, he poured his kiss into her until their rapid breathing came together and he could feel every silken inch of her with the front of his body.

A keen breeze rattled the roof of the shed. It might have been the sound that brought him back, or perhaps some inner thermostat of his own, but he became aware suddenly that he was going to take her here in old man Jaroch's toolshed. And then he thought, Oh, Christ, how hard have I been holding her? His own muscles ached from the force, and he brought his head up to examine her upturned face. Sleepy lashes dusted her cheeks. A contented smile curved over damp and swollen lips. Her skin was lustrous. He pulled her into the curve of his arm with a relieved sigh, cradling her while he tried to contain his overwhelming appetite. Not here, Ludan. Not like this, with half your mind on freeze.

Kissing her once on each eyelid, he steeled his self-restraint and put her very gently from him. Her eyes flew open; her gaze leaped curiously to his.

"Heart of my heart, I'm sorry," he said softly, smiling at her, "but if I don't take my shameless hands off you . . ."

"I might end up experiencing the fullness of my woman-hood in a toolshed?" she finished for him. Her returning grin had a sexy sweetness that tested his resolution. "It's not the worst idea I've ever heard."

But it is, Chris, he thought. Because enough of me hasn't walked out of that cell yet to make what would happen between us into an act of love. And the trust I see in your eyes would never allow me to give you less.

OFFICIAL RULES

To enter the sweepstakes below carefully follow all instructions found elsewhere in this offer.

The **Winners Classic** will award prizes with the following approximate maximum values: 1 Grand Prize: $26,500 (or $25,000 cash alternate); 1 First Prize: $3,000; 5 Second Prizes: $400 each; 35 Third Prizes: $100 each; 1,000 Fourth Prizes: $7.50 each. Total maximum retail value of Winners Classic Sweepstakes is $42,500. Some presentations of this sweepstakes may contain individual entry numbers corresponding to one or more of the aforementioned prize levels. To determine the Winners, individual entry numbers will first be compared with the winning numbers preselected by computer. For winning numbers not returned, prizes will be awarded in random drawings from among all eligible entries received. Prize choices may be offered at various levels. If a winner chooses an automobile prize, all license and registration fees, taxes, destination charges and, other expenses not offered herein are the responsibility of the winner. If a winner chooses a trip, travel must be complete within one year from the time the prize is awarded. Minors must be accompanied by an adult. Travel companion(s) must also sign release of liability. Trips are subject to space and departure availability. Certain black-out dates may apply.

The following applies to the sweepstakes named above:

No purchase necessary. You can also enter the sweepstakes by sending your name and address to: P.O. Box 508, Gibbstown, N.J. 08027. Mail each entry separately. Sweepstakes begins 6/1/93. Entries must be received by 12/30/94. Not responsible for lost, late, damaged, misdirected, illegible or postage due mail. Mechanically reproduced entries are not eligible. All entries become property of the sponsor and will not be returned.

Prize Selection/Validations: Selection of winners will be conducted no later than 5:00 PM on January 28, 1995, by an independent judging organization whose decisions are final. Random drawings will be held at 1211 Avenue of the Americas, New York, N.Y. 10036. Entrants need not be present to win. Odds of winning are determined by total number of entries received. Circulation of this sweepstakes is estimated not to exceed 200 million. All prizes are guaranteed to be awarded and delivered to winners. Winners will be notified by mail and may be required to complete an affidavit of eligibility and release of liability which must be returned within 14 days of date on notification or alternate winners will be selected in a random drawing. Any prize notification letter or any prize returned to a participating sponsor, Bantam Doubleday Dell Publishing Group, Inc., its participating divisions or subsidiaries, or the independent judging organization as undeliverable will be awarded to an alternate winner. Prizes are not transferable. No substitution for prizes except as offered or as may be necessary due to unavailability, in which case a prize of equal or greater value will be awarded. Prizes will be awarded approximately 90 days after the drawing. All taxes are the sole responsibility of the winners. Entry constitutes permission (except where prohibited by law) to use winners' names, hometowns, and likenesses for publicity purposes without further or other compensation. Prizes won by minors will be awarded in the name of parent or legal guardian.

Participation: Sweepstakes open to residents of the United States and Canada, except for the province of Quebec. Sweepstakes sponsored by Bantam Doubleday Dell Publishing Group, Inc., (BDD), 1540 Broadway, New York, NY 10036. Versions of this sweepstakes with different graphics and prize choices will be offered in conjunction with various solicitations or promotions by different subsidiaries and divisions of BDD. Where applicable, winners will have their choice of any prize offered at level won. Employees of BDD, its divisions, subsidiaries, advertising agencies, independent judging organization, and their immediate family members are not eligible.

Canadian residents, in order to win, must first correctly answer a time limited arithmetical skill testing question. Void in Puerto Rico, Quebec and wherever prohibited or restricted by law. Subject to all federal, state, local and provincial laws and regulations. For a list of major prize winners (available after 1/29/95): send a self-addressed, stamped envelope entirely separate from your entry to: Sweepstakes Winners, P.O. Box 517, Gibbstown, NJ 08027. Requests must be received by 12/30/94. DO NOT SEND ANY OTHER CORRESPONDENCE TO THIS P.O. BOX.

SWP 7/93